Wa
Da

She realized suddenly that Rowan was surveying the expanse of thigh her skimpy outfit revealed.

"I...I'd better get dressed," she stammered.

His eyes darkened as he took a step toward her. "I suppose you'd better—" his voice carried little conviction "—but on the other hand..."

"There is no other hand," she said determinedly. Spellbound by his gaze, Danni was finding it hard to remember her vow not to ever become involved with any man of Trina's, past or present.

Rowan's finger traced a line down her face as he asked, "Are you sure?"

An anguished moan escaped her lips. How could she ever be sure whom he was really seeing when he looked at her?

Valerie Parv had a busy and successful career as a journalist and advertising copywriter before she began writing for Harlequin in 1982. She is an enthusiastic member of several Australian writers' organizations. Her many interests include her husband, her cat and the Australian environment. Her love of the land is a distinguishing feature in many of her books for Harlequin. She has recently written a colorful study in a non-fiction book title *The Changing Face of Australia*. Her home is in New South Wales.

Books by Valerie Parv

Centrefold
Valerie Parv

Harlequin Books

TORONTO • NEW YORK • LONDON
AMSTERDAM • PARIS • SYDNEY • HAMBURG
STOCKHOLM • ATHENS • TOKYO • MILAN

Original hardcover edition published in 1988
by Mills & Boon Limited

ISBN 0-373-02969-1

Harlequin Romance first edition March 1989

CHAPTER ONE

DANNI O'DARE scanned the completed application form, pleased that she could show she was amply qualified for the journalist's position she sought. But would the publisher of Monarch Magazines agree? For the sake of her dwindling savings, she hoped so.

She handed the form to the publisher's secretary and reached into her briefcase. 'I brought along some samples of my published work as well.'

The secretary nodded. 'Good. You'll need them for the interview.' Her intercom buzzed and she leaned towards it. 'Yes, Mr Monarch?'

'Give Danielle O'Dare my apologies, will you? I can't see her for another half-hour. Something just came up.'

'Yes, sir.' She looked at Danni, her expression apologetic. 'I take it you heard? Can you wait?'

Danni's spirits plummeted. After her disappointing week, she was starting to wonder whether she still had a career left. Having to wait strained her nerves to the limit, but she forced herself to smile. 'I don't mind. Is there somewhere I can wait?'

'Usually you could stay here, but until the decorating is finished, we don't have a reception area. On the next floor there's a cafeteria where you might get a cup of coffee.'

Gingerly, Danni picked her way through the debris of new carpets and furnishings, and headed for the lift. On every side, she was surrounded by the familiar sounds of a newspaper office, except that the clack of typewriters had been replaced by the click of video display terminals, and the rustle of paper had become the flicker of video screens. All the same, it was her world, and she hoped her interview today would make her a part of it again.

When she reached the cafeteria, she was surprised to find it deserted. There wasn't even a coffee machine from which she could help herself. She looked at the spotless tables with their upended chairs. It was obvious that she couldn't wait here.

The sound of voices further along the corridor caught her attention and she followed it, cautiously pushing open a door. She found herself in a photographic studio and slid quietly into a chair near the door. Surely no one would mind if she observed the session? After all, she was hoping to come to work here.

With professional interest, she studied the scene in front of her. They were apparently working on a fashion spread with an autumn theme. Although it was late spring outside, the models were dressed in trans-seasonal clothes and carried umbrellas as props. At one side of the tawny cyclorama on which the girls posed, a powerful fan blew an autumn 'breeze' into their faces.

Danni regarded the shivering models with sympathy. As a journalist, she had never envied the girls on the other side of the camera, knowing that their work was not as easy or glamorous as it appeared to be. Her twin sister's career was proof of that.

As she thought of Trina, a fresh wave of gloom clouded Danni's normally vivacious features. Much as she hated to admit it, it was largely because of Trina that Danni was job-hunting today.

As assistant editor of an influential investment magazine, she had thought she was secure for the foreseeable future. But, one week ago, everything had changed...

She had known something was wrong as soon as she arrived at her office and sensed the tension in the air. 'It's Trina again, isn't it?' she asked her editor, Ray Conreid, when he summoned her to his office.

He frowned. 'I'm afraid so. Look, I know you two can't help looking so alike, but sometimes I wish you were more like chalk and cheese, then I wouldn't be in the dilemma I am right now.'

'What's the matter?' she asked resignedly.

'It's the publisher. Mrs Philmont is such a stickler for the proprieties, as you know, and she does own this magazine. Well, she just found out about your sister's latest escapade, and she read the riot act to me on the phone this morning.'

'Surely you told her it wasn't me in the magazine?'

'I told her, repeatedly. She says that isn't the point. The fact is, her subscribers *think* it's you, and they aren't going to give much credence to investment advice written by a ... a nude centrefold.'

'So she told you to fire me, is that it?'

'I told her how unfair it was.'

Danni's eyes flashed fire. 'Then I'll save you the trouble, Ray. I'll resign as of this morning.'

Ray tried unsuccessfully to mask his relief. 'You needn't resign. This will probably blow over soon.'

'But not soon enough for Mrs Philmont. Don't worry, Ray, I've been thinking of changing jobs, anyway. So you go ahead and tell Mrs P that you did your duty. I'll be fine, honestly.'

'It still seems unfair,' he grumbled, but she noticed that he didn't try to make her change her mind. He offered her a fortnight's salary in lieu of notice, and wished her well even as he ushered her out of his office.

When the decision was made, she felt strangely relieved. She had been tiring of the financial scene, but hadn't done anything about it. Now the decision had been made for her and she was almost glad. She was only sorry that she had just taken her annual holidays. The extra cash would have given her more time to look around. But at least she would have the two weeks' pay in hand.

Three hours later, having cleaned out her desk and briefed the other journalist on the stories she'd been covering, she walked out of the office into unemployment.

Monarch Magazines was her third interview this week. She preferred not to think about the first two. Surely not everyone in Sydney thought she was this month's centrefold girl? The first two editors who had interviewed her evidently did, and their suggestive comments had warned her what to expect if she went to work for them. She hoped that today's interview would concentrate more on her writing skills and less on her supposed physical charms.

With an effort, she focused her attention on the scene in front of her. She could only see the photographer in silhouette but he was tall and powerfully built. He was also a perfectionist, judging by the way he was ordering the models around.

'Come on, Margo, you're supposed to be a society belle out strolling in the park, not a street girl waiting on a corner,' he exploded.

'There's no need to be insulting,' the model retorted, but Danni noticed that she tried harder to please the photographer.

'That's better. Put your head back a little more. Eyes wide. Fake it, darling, fake it,' he coaxed.

He had a nice voice when he spoke pleasantly, Danni noticed idly. It reminded her of warm honey running off a spoon. It was a pity he didn't seem to have the manners to match his voice.

'That's the girl. Hold it. Now, swirl the skirt around a little more. And again. Got it!' While he was speaking, he was working the camera, shooting high and low as the models followed his directions.

'OK, girls, that's it for today.'

The models stepped off the cyclorama, shedding their autumn coats until they were revealed in bright spring dresses. Suddenly Danni was dazzled as the arc lights were turned off and the room lights came on overhead. Self-consciously, she shrank back in her seat, but no one paid her any attention.

'Where the hell is what's-her-name, the one with the hands?' the photographer asked his assistant irritably.

The younger man had his back to Danni, but she saw him consult his watch. 'She was booked for right after the autumn shots, so she must be running late.'

'Why can't these women take the trouble to be on time?' the photographer grumbled. He swung around and Danni saw his face for the first time. Unwillingly, she drew a sharp breath of admiration.

Arrogant and demanding he might be, but he was also disturbingly attractive. His dark, hawkish profile might have come straight out of Lawrence of Arabia. His powerful build contrasted with the delicate way he handled the expensive cameras and lighting equipment. In the full glare of the studio lights, his tanned skin glowed almost bronze. His intriguingly contoured face was framed by glossy blue-black hair which just grazed his collar and speared to chisel-shaped sideburns on either side of his face.

While looking her fill at him, she was unprepared when he turned the full intensity of his gaze on her. 'How long have you been sitting there?'

'Me?' she squeaked, surprise almost robbing her of her voice.

He sighed theatrically. 'Who do you think I mean? Well, since you're here, you may as well make yourself useful.'

Instinctively, she gathered her legs under her, ready for a quick escape. 'In what way?'

He gave another sigh. 'You just heard Tony explain that my "hands" haven't turned up for the ring shots. You've got good hands, so you may as well stand in.'

Since her hands were clamped tightly around her attaché case, how did he know what sort of hands she had? She shook her head. 'No, I can't.'

His eyes narrowed. 'You mean you won't. I suppose you think you can just breeze in here and sit on the sidelines, as if this was a show for your entertainment.'

What on earth had she done to make him so angry with her? 'I didn't think anything of the sort,' she defended herself. 'I didn't have anywhere else to go.'

'Bloody typical,' he said angrily. He turned away to where his assistant was throwing a black velvet cloth over a table, presumably for the jewellery photographs he was so uptight about.

Before he could pillory her further, she was saved by the arrival of the editor's secretary. 'Ah, there you are! I'd forgotten that they close the cafeteria in the afternoons these days, or I'd have found somewhere else for you to wait. But I'm glad you found something useful to occupy your time.'

'I'd hardly call it useful,' she heard the photographer sneer as she hurried out with the secretary.

On the way to the lift, she fought to regain control of her breathing, which was fast and shallow after her unpleasant encounter.

'Do you know Rowan Traynor, then?' the secretary asked.

'Hardly. I think he objected to having an audience. He was angry because I wouldn't let him use my hands in one of his photographs.'

The secretary raised her eyebrows. 'Do you know how many women would give their eye-teeth to be photographed by him?'

'Well, I'm not one of them.' Danni was thankful that the lift arrived just then. One encounter with the arrogant Mr Traynor was quite enough, without going on and on about it.

But the secretary persisted. 'He's quite famous, you know. He's photographed heaps of celebrities, published books, you name it. I'm surprised you haven't heard of him.'

'I've been in financial journalism,' Danni explained, then wished she had kept quiet. She didn't want to prejudice her chances of getting a job here.

Fortunately, the secretary let the remark pass without comment, and Danni was soon shaking hands with the head of Monarch Magazines.

To her relief, he was a fatherly-looking man with a shock of silvery hair. But her relief was short-lived when she saw the flicker of recognition in his eyes.

Motioning her to sit, he cleared his throat and regarded her curiously. 'I understood you were a journalist, Miss O'Dare.'

'That's right. I have a B-grading and some experience as an acting editor,' she said firmly.

'Then you must model part-time.'

'I don't model at all, although I have a twin sister who does. I may be reminding you of her.'

He stared at her over the rim of his reading-glasses. 'I must say, the resemblance is remarkable.'

Here we go again, she thought miserably. She was sure that Mr Monarch had seen the centrefold and was mentally comparing her with it. He probably didn't believe she had a twin sister. Why, oh, why did Trina have to go and model nude? It was bad enough when she posed provocatively for lingerie advertisements, but this was the limit. Not for the first time, Danni wished their parents hadn't decided to take up a legacy in Ireland. Under Sean O'Dare's eye, Trina wouldn't have dared to do such a thing.

Danni became aware that Mr Monarch was speaking to her. 'I'm sorry, my mind was wandering.'

'Hardly a good thing in a journalist,' he observed. 'I asked whether you had any experience of reporting for the women's pages.'

She explained about her background, adding that she had spent her cadetship on a women's magazine. 'In any case, I understood that you were planning a life-style magazine,' she added.

He smiled dismissively. 'Life-style, women's pages—it's all the same thing. "Fifty different ways with mince." Frankly, I don't think it would suit you.'

So that was that. She rose smoothly and gathered up the samples he hadn't even asked to see. 'Thank you for your time, Mr Monarch.'

He forestalled her with a gesture. 'Just a moment, Miss O'Dare. Perhaps we do have something for you.'

Her hopes rose fleetingly. 'Yes?'

'I've been thinking of starting a modern men's magazine, a sort of male fantasy thing. We could use you in its pages, if you're interested.'

With an effort, she kept her smile intact. 'I've already explained that I'm a writer, not a model.'

As she walked out, she saw him reach into a desk drawer and take out a magazine which was folded over at the spine. She imagined him unfolding the glossy centre spread and shaking his head over it, no doubt asking himself what sort of fool she took him for.

It was only when she was outside in the fresh air again that the humour of the situation struck her. If Mr Monarch thought he could disguise outdated 'women's pages' fare as a new magazine, he was in for a shock. She might not have had much contact with the fashion scene, but Danni knew her own kind. Fifty different ways with mince, indeed! She was glad she wouldn't be working for him.

The discovery added a spring to her step as she headed for the station. Passers-by smiled at her involuntarily as she smiled back, unaware that they weren't delighting in the glorious weather as much as in her response to it. Her unusual height, close to six feet, gave her an appealingly coltish look as she stepped out, and her ash-blonde hair, which she wore in a bob level with her earlobes, moved and swayed as she walked.

Gradually, she became aware that a car had slowed to a crawl and was keeping pace with her. She gave it a nervous, sideways glance, trying to appear unconcerned. She gained a quick impression of a metallic-silver sports car, a Mercedes, she thought, but wasn't sure. However, she did recognise the driver in the split second before she looked away. It was the photographer from the magazine.

Determinedly, she ignored him and kept walking. At the next corner, she stopped to wait for the lights to change, and the photographer eased his car into the kerb beside her. Reaching across, he opened the passenger door. 'Jump in, darling, and I'll give you a lift home.'

'No, thank you,' she said stiffly, still avoiding his gaze.

Out of the corner of her eye, she saw him frown. 'What's come over you? Playing hard to get?'

The nerve of the man! He might well be famous and have every woman in town at his feet but, as she had told the secretary, she wasn't one of them. 'Will you kindly leave me alone?' she muttered. The other people waiting at the crossing gave her a startled glance, then looked away.

He shrugged. 'Have it your way, darling. See you around.'

Not if she could help it, she vowed as he drove away. All the same, as she sat in the train, she couldn't help wondering what would have happened if she had accepted his offer of a lift. He was obviously attracted to her, even though they'd only spent those few minutes together in the studio. Why else would he follow her?

She wondered where he was headed. He looked the type to spend his evenings at parties, surrounded by beautiful women. On the other hand, he also looked as if he would enjoy an intimate dinner for two at a dimly lit restaurant, having discovered the place weeks ahead of the restaurant columnists.

She had a sudden vision of herself seated opposite him, their wine glasses touching as they gazed into each other's eyes. Goodness, she was almost as bad as he was, making assumptions about someone she barely knew!

She was glad when the train pulled into her home station of Waverton and she could walk the short but hilly way home. After their parents returned to Ireland, she and Trina had discussed sharing a flat. Now, she was glad they had decided to have their own places. Trina lived in a nearby suburb and was a frequent visitor, but it would have been a strain living together. Despite their looks, they were very different people, and there were times, like this evening, when Danni looked forward to an evening of her own company.

But no sooner had she dropped her briefcase in the bedroom and kicked off her shoes than the doorbell rang. 'Oh, it's you,' she said ungraciously as she opened the door to her twin sister.

Over Trina's shoulder, she saw a delivery man doing a double-take as he crossed the hall. She smiled. She and Trina were accustomed to the attention their identical looks attracted, but it still amused her to see the startled reactions they drew. As usual, Danni noted, her twin was impeccably made-up and dressed in the latest fashions which, she was aware, made her own businesslike suit and subdued make-up seem lacklustre by comparison. Normally, Danni took pride in Trina's glossy appearance, but today it only reminded her of why she was unemployed right now. 'You'd better come in,' she said, almost as an afterthought.

Trina pouted prettily. 'I only came over to commiserate with you, and I brought dinner.'

She thrust a pair of shopping bags into Danni's arms. 'What have you got in here?' she asked, noting the weight.

'All the ingredients to make *sukiyaki*,' Trina explained.

'You *are* getting fancy. What's the occasion?'

'Unemployed people sometimes neglect themselves. I didn't want it to happen to you,' Trina said seriously.

'But I've only been out of work for a week, and I've already been to three interviews,' Danni protested.

Trina's eyebrows lifted. 'How did it go today?'

Danni grimaced. 'A repeat of the first two. Mr Monarch is an appalling male chauvinist who didn't believe I had a twin sister who modelled.'

'And he thought you were the centrefold girl?' Danni nodded, and Trina's mouth tightened in annoyance. 'But that's not fair. In any case, isn't that discrimination or something? Can't you sue him?'

A wave of weariness washed over Danni. 'I wouldn't bother with him. I didn't even want to work for him, come to that. So don't worry, there'll be plenty of other jobs.'

'Sure, but what will you do for rent money until they come along?'

At the reminder, Danni sobered. 'I'll manage, I suppose. I just wish I hadn't taken such an expensive holiday.'

'You didn't know how things would work out. But at least three weeks in Fiji has given you a super suntan.'

Trina led the way into the kitchen and started to unpack the ingredients for the *sukiyaki*, while Danni got out her cast-iron wok.

Then they divided the task of chopping the ingredients between them, until Danni broke the companionable silence with a chuckle.

Trina's head came up. 'What's so funny?'

'I was just thinking. When I left Monarch Magazines this afternoon, one of their photographers tried to pick me up.'

Trina didn't seem surprised. 'Was it anyone I know?'

'You mean, they're all like that?'

'Not all, but I have met a few. What was this one's name?'

Danni had a mental block. 'Let's see, Roland, or something. I did notice that he drives a sports car.'

There was a long pause before Trina said, 'It doesn't give me much to go on. Can you describe him?'

To her astonishment, Danni found that she could remember every line of the man's disturbingly attractive face, down to the blue-black hair and chisel-shaped sideburns. If she admitted as much, Trina would have her paired off in no time, so she kept her thoughts to herself. 'It doesn't really matter.'

'Then you're not going to see him again?' Trina sounded disappointed.

An unwanted frisson of excitement travelled down Danni's spine at the idea, but she suppressed it. 'Not if I can help it! He was rude and presumptuous, assuming I'd accept a lift from someone I'd hardly met.'

'He sounds like quite a man.'

'Maybe, but I prefer men to treat me as a person, not some kind of sex object.'

Trina held up her hands in mock-surrender. 'Easy, girl, I was only asking.'

Danni felt foolish. 'I didn't mean to get so worked up.' It was just that the very thought of the man disturbed her, she mused, at the same time wondering why such a casual encounter should have left her feeling so defensive.

Fortunately, Trina was happy to change the subject and they ate their *sukiyaki* in between a heated discussion about a film they had both seen recently. It was only when they were about to have coffee that Danni realised she had been doing most of the talking for some time. 'Is anything the matter, Trina?' she asked as she carried the coffee percolator and cups to the living-room.

Trina looked down at the table, but not before Danni spotted the twin patches of colour staining her cheeks. 'What is it?' she asked heavily, a feeling of foreboding overtaking her.

'It's nothing,' Trina insisted.

Danni was tempted to accept her sister's assurance, but she knew Trina as well as she knew herself. There was something bothering her, and it was only a matter of time before she shared it with

Danni. The problem, whatever it was, was probably what had brought her here tonight.

'Come on, what is it?' she repeated.

'I...haven't been feeling too well lately,' Trina began with seeming reluctance.

Danni's heart sank. 'You look fine,' she ventured, knowing it wouldn't help.

Trina sighed. 'I know, and there's nothing I can put my finger on, really. Perhaps I've just been working too hard. I feel as if I should go away somewhere quiet for a few days.'

'Then for goodness' sake, go,' Danni urged. 'There's nothing stopping you, is there?'

'I'm afraid there is. I'm booked for a rather lengthy assignment next week.'

'Can't you cancel it?'

Trina shook her head. 'I wish I could, but it's an important client. If I cancel out at such short notice, the agency could drop me from their books. I'd find it nearly impossible to get a new agent, once word got around that I was unreliable.'

Danni sympathised with her twin's dilemma, but could see no solution. 'It looks like you'll have to complete the assignment and then take your holiday.'

Tears of self-pity welled in Trina's large, expressive eyes. 'I know. I'd already arrived at the same conclusion.'

'It's a pity that I'm not a model, after all, or I could take your place,' Danni joked, trying to lighten the atmosphere.

She was unprepared for Trina's enthusiastic response. 'Oh, Danni, could you do it? It would be the perfect solution. You could keep the fee to tide you over until you get a job, and I could take the break I need.'

Jolting her coffee-cup down on to the table, Danni clenched her hands together. 'Now, just a minute! I only said it as a joke. I don't know the first thing about modelling. I'd make a complete idiot of myself, and probably ruin your career into the bargain.'

'No, you wouldn't. You're a natural, and I could coach you on the details. You've already said that everybody thinks you're me, anyway. Who would know the difference?'

'I would,' Danni said. How could Trina even suggest such a thing? It was true, they had sometimes traded places when they were children, but that had been harmless fun. This was different. 'I couldn't,' she repeated.

Trina lowered her head. 'I suppose it was too much to ask. I'll just have to do it and hope the chest pains don't get any worse.'

Her defeated tone alarmed Danni. 'What chest pains?'

'It's nothing to worry about. A recurrence of the old problem, I expect. Forget it.'

'Have you been to the doctor?'

Trina nodded. 'He says there's a virus going around. It wouldn't worry most people, but with my lungs...' Her voice trailed off.

Danni knew she was trapped. How could she let Trina undertake an assignment which might injure her health, when she was responsible for the scar tissue clouding her twin's lungs?

If only they hadn't gone sailing on their sixteenth birthday. But they had, and a swinging boom had knocked Danni overboard, stunning her as she sank like a stone. Suffering from a cold, Trina had dived repeatedly until she found Danni and brought her to shore, saving her life. Apart from a headache, Danni had suffered no ill-effects, but Trina's cold had turned into pneumonia. Her recovery had required months of rest and treatment, and had left her with scarred lungs, so she was prey to every chest infection going.

All because of me, Danni remembered. How did one ever repay a debt like that? 'Very well, I'll do it,' she said. At the same time, she knew she had been manipulated by Trina, and wondered how many more times she would be called upon to repay her twin for saving her life.

Trina brightened at once. 'You won't regret your decision. It's a very lucrative job.'

She named a fee which made Danni choke on her coffee. 'They pay as much as that?'

'Not usually, but this is a special assignment.'

Suspicion welled in Danni's mind. 'It isn't another centrefold, is it?'

'Would I do that to you? No, you'll be modelling a new collection of Australian swimwear for an overseas catalogue.'

'Swimwear? I don't know about that.'

'You'll be fine. You look fantastic in a bikini, at least as good as me,' Trina added immodestly. 'Look at it this way. At least you'll be wearing *something!* And everyone will think you're me, so your own reputation will be untarnished.'

Put like that, it seemed churlish to think of refusing, but Danni felt distinctly uneasy, although she nodded her head. 'All right, if you're sure no one will know the difference.'

'Of course they won't. It will be compensation for you, after all the trouble I caused you with my centrefold. This time, you'll be beating them at their own game.'

She made it sound so easy, Danni thought, but the prospect of parading in front of a camera filled her with dread. Remembering the arrogant way the photographer treated the models at Monarch Magazines this afternoon, she shuddered. If anyone treated her like that, she would be tempted to retaliate in kind. And she doubted whether a man like Roland . . . no, she had it now, *Rowan* Traynor, would appreciate a dose of his own medicine.

'Where will the photographs be taken?' she asked Trina.

'Most of them will be shot in a new studio at North Sydney. I'll give you all the details over the weekend. Then there'll be some location shooting, probably at Bondi Beach.'

Trina hadn't mentioned that the job would involve posing on a public beach. 'I'm not sure about this,' she said as her doubts returned.

Trina squeezed her hand. 'Relax. After you've had a taste of being a celebrity, with people craning their necks to recognise you on the beach at Bondi, you won't want to go back to being Danielle O'Dare, girl reporter. Which reminds me, you'll have to get used to being called Miss Dare.'

'I keep forgetting you drop the "O" from your professional name,' Danni observed. 'I'll have a lot to get used to in a hurry.'

'I told you, I'll coach you so stop worrying.'

All the same, Danni *did* worry. It was all very well for Trina to dismiss it lightly, but masquerading as someone else did not come easily to Danni. If she hadn't owed Trina so much, she wouldn't even consider it. As it was, her heart raced at the very thought of what she was agreeing to do. Only Trina's unshakeable confidence gave her courage. She squared her shoulders determinedly and gave her twin a shaky smile.

'All right, where do we start?'

CHAPTER TWO

'MAKE sure you keep your temper in check. Models are supposed to be seen and not heard.'

Trina's last bit of advice was still ringing in Danni's ears as she prepared to leave for the photographic studio. Her only consolation was how much happier Trina had looked when she had left last night for her short vacation.

They had worked all weekend to turn Danni from a journalist into something approaching a model, and although Trina swore the transformation was complete, Danni still felt horribly unsure. Only the sight of her twin's face and listless demeanour had spurred her to go through with this. Trina really looked as if she needed the break, and she had been pathetically grateful when she'd left last night.

'You're sure you don't mind?' she had asked over and over.

'Of course not. Now go and get some rest! I'll take care of everything.' How often had she said that since they were children? Danni mused as she put the finishing touches to her make-up. The kohl eye-liner and several shades of shadow merging into one another felt heavy and strange, accustomed as she was to wearing the lightest foundation and lip-gloss. But Trina had assured her she would be expected to turn up in full professional make-up.

'Damn!' she swore softly as her mascara-coated lash left a smudge on one cheek. Her hands were trembling. Making an effort to steady them, she wiped away the offending mark and strained her eyes wide to re-apply the mascara. There, that was better.

'Ready, Miss O'D...Miss Dare?' she asked, forcing a smile to her lips as she confronted her reflection. 'Not a chance!' she muttered, turning away. As she gathered her things, she recalled the instruction the Monarch photographer had given to the model—fake it. That was what she would have to do: pretend to be confident and assured, even though she was quaking inwardly.

She located the address Trina had given her easily enough. It was in Milson's Point, in an expensive-looking, harbour-front building which had evidently once housed residential apartments, but was now given over to business—mainly advertising agencies, art studios and film-makers. A hand-lettered sign pointed the way to the 'Photographic Studio' up a flight of stairs off the lobby. Evidently the studio had only recently moved into the building, since their name wasn't yet listed on the tenants' notice-board.

Her heart was thudding alarmingly as she mounted the two flights, following the hand-written signs. They ended at a flamboyant purple door, and she stood in front of it, taking deep breaths to calm herself.

'Fake it,' she reminded herself, and tried to conjure up some of Trina's insouciance. It was only partly successful, and she found herself wishing for a tough interview subject; a hostile politician or one of the many senior businessmen she'd interviewed. Anything was better than this awful sensation of stepping into an abyss.

She almost turned and ran when the door swung open just as she was reaching for the handle. 'Hello,' she said huskily to the smiling young man who stood there. He was casually dressed in slim-fitting jeans and a checked shirt, and looked to be in his early twenties.

'Hello, again,' he said, his eyes sweeping over her/Trina's outfit of aqua-satin trousers and creamy lace over-blouse. 'You don't remember me, do you? Anthony McGuire.'

'Of course,' she lied, holding out her hand. 'Nice to see you again . . . er . . . Anthony. Were you going out? I can come back later.'

'We're a bit low on milk for the coffee,' he explained, 'so I thought I'd dash out and get some. But since you're here, we may as well get started. Time is money, as they say. Come on in.'

His manner was so easy and natural that she found herself relaxing. Maybe this wasn't going to be so bad, after all.

The studio was enormous, taking up most of its floor of the building. Floor-to-ceiling windows filled the wall facing her, and offered a breathtaking view of the harbour all the way to the city centre, with Centrepoint Tower rising like a steel mushroom out of a cluster of other skyscrapers. The windows were flanked by heavy black curtains on an electrically operated track—to enable the photographer to control the amount of light coming in, she guessed.

To her right was a massive white cyclorama, suspended from a rod fixed to the ceiling. Behind it were mounted several huge rolls of paper in different colours, ready to be unrolled to provide any background colour desired. In front of that was the usual battery of cameras and lighting equipment which Danni had encountered when she had worked with photographers in the past. Her pulses began to slow reassuringly. She felt much more at home here than she had expected to.

'You have a very nice set-up here,' she commented in what she trusted was an imitation of Trina's light tones.

'Thanks. We've only been here a couple of weeks, but we're starting to get the place into shape. Coffee?'

'No, thanks. I... I'd rather get to work.' And get this over with, she added to herself.

He hesitated for a moment. 'But... well, I suppose you could get into the first outfit. They're all in that corner.'

She followed his outstretched arm to a rack of swimwear covered by clear plastic sheeting. 'Where do I change?' she asked, looking around for signs of another room.

He grinned. 'It'll have to be right here, I'm afraid. We haven't set up the changing-rooms yet. They're next week's job. I know it's a pest having to leave everything on the floor, but it will be different next time you come, I promise.'

He thought her look of dismay was because there was nowhere to hang her street clothes, she realised. He couldn't know that it was at the prospect of changing in the same room as a strange man, which a real model would take in her stride. She knew they did, because she had seen the girls blithely shedding their clothes in the middle of crowded rooms. Except that, on those occasions, it wasn't *her* body that was on public exhibition.

'Here goes nothing,' she muttered under her breath, walking unsteadily towards the corner.

Over her shoulder, she noted that Anthony was occupied with setting up lights and reflectors around the cyclorama, so she quickly pushed the clothes rack across the corner to partially shield her from the rest of the room. In this makeshift hide-out, she stripped off her satin trousers and the lace top.

Each swimsuit had a number pinned to it, so she slid number one off its padded hanger and held it up. It was her size, or rather, Trina's, since the client would have known her twin's measurements when they booked her. But there was so little of the suit: only narrow satin cups linked by pieces of gold chain. A triangle of satin with gold chains at the sides comprised the bottom half of the suit.

Before her courage deserted her altogether, she unhooked her bra and slid the bikini top on. It was underwired to thrust her full breasts forward, forming a deep cleft between them, and she looked at the results with alarm. She looked like a Hollywood sweater girl without the sweater!

The bottom half was barely decent, and then only if worn in one's own bedroom, she thought, snapping the gold chains into the loops at each side. Whoever designed this thing obviously didn't intend to get wet. It would probably dissolve at the sight of water!

There was an art deco mirror on the wall to one side of her, and she bent to it to comb her hair. Behind her, she heard the sound of the studio door opening and a deep male voice said, 'Hi! How's it going, Tony?' In the act of thrusting the comb through her hair, she froze. Oh, no! She would know that throaty voice anywhere. Rowan Traynor. He must be the photographer taking the shots—not Anthony McGuire, as she'd assumed. Then it came to her, Anthony was the Tony she'd glimpsed assisting Rowan Traynor at Monarch last week. She hadn't seen his face, just his back as he worked.

Trina must have known that Rowan was to be the photographer when she arranged all this. How could she do it after what Danni had said about disliking Rowan's type?

Nervousness made her fumble as she tried to adjust the back fastening of the bikini top, and she stood transfixed as capable hands took the flimsy material from her and began to fasten it. Then the hands slid over her bare shoulders and down her arms. Not knowing how Trina would have reacted to this, she said nothing, but her breathing grew increasingly laboured as he massaged her flesh.

'That's much better,' he said softly into her ear. 'I'm glad you're over your touch-me-not mood.'

He must be referring to their first encounter at Monarch Magazines. He had evidently mistaken her for Trina on that occasion as well, which at least explained his presumptuous behaviour. Her shrug was carefully non-committal. 'You know me— changeable as the wind.' Which was certainly true of her twin's moods.

Gently, he turned her to face him, and she gasped as her eyes met his intensely blue ones. She had never encountered such a disturbingly direct gaze before, and she felt naked under his scrutiny. Surely her deception must be revealed to such a searching inspection?

He was half a head taller than she was, putting his lips on a level with her eyes so she was achingly conscious of the inviting fullness of them. They parted into a half-smile, and his head bent forward until she was sure he meant to kiss her. Unaccountably, her pulses began to race and she felt hot colour surging to her cheeks. Good God! Surely she didn't want him to kiss her?

Just as she was braced for the onslaught of his embrace, he turned abruptly away. 'Let's get to work, Trina,' he said.

A wave of something akin to disappointment washed over her. He alarmed and intrigued her, and she should be thankful that she had escaped his amorous attentions, even though they were intended for Trina, not her. Instead, she felt like a child who had been promised a treat, only to have it snatched away at the last moment.

He was adjusting the setting on his camera when she emerged from her makeshift enclosure, and he looked up as she walked across, remembering to swivel her hips in the provocative way Trina had taught her. Anthony whistled softly, but Rowan watched impassively then returned to his camera.

When he looked up again, it was to gesture towards the backdrop, against which Tony had set up a grove of plastic trees with a mesh hammock slung between them. Actually, the hammock was braced on steel poles, but they were out of camera range, behind the trees. As she eased herself on to the hammock, it bounced and swayed alarmingly beneath her.

'Keep one foot on the ground and it won't move so much,' Rowan advised.

Obediently, she draped one leg over the side of the hammock, which steadied under her. The position felt awfully unnatural, but she assumed it looked effective through the camera lens.

'Right, let's see the head back and those eyes wide,' he instructed. 'Flirt with me, Trina. Invite me to bed with your eyes.'

Did he have to put it like that? she thought irritably, but recalled Trina's injunction about keeping hold of her temper. She widened her eyes and fluttered her lashes at him, arching her neck backwards as instructed.

'If that's sexy, I'm Robert Redford,' he growled. 'For God's sake, relax, girl! You're as stiff as a lump of wood.'

She thought she *was* relaxed, but made an effort to loosen her limbs even more. The muscles in her back began to protest at the awkward pose and she moved slightly to ease them.

'Freeze, can't you?' Rowan barked. 'This isn't a movie we're shooting, you know.'

'I know,' she snapped back, and saw his eyebrows lift. She amended quickly, 'I'm sorry. Is this better?'

'A little. Now, lift your leg and let it swing free. I know the hammock's moving, but I'll worry about

that. Raise your leg. Higher. Now, ruffle your hair
with your free hand.'

She felt like a puppet being jerked this way and
that as he pulled the strings. At first she tried to
follow his directions, then became so confused that
she started moving a leg when he meant an arm,
and ended up in a hopeless tangle. 'I'm sorry,' she
said abjectly as he swore under his breath.

'You should be,' he snapped. 'I've seen some
useless women in my time, but you're heading for
the prize.'

This was one of the kinder things he said to her!
As she changed into one garment after another,
moving and posing in each one, she began to
wonder if he was deliberately trying to make her
lose her temper. She couldn't believe he spoke to
his models like this as a matter of course. Even the
scene she'd witnessed at Monarch Magazines wasn't
as bad as this. If he was baiting her, he was in for
a surprise. The more he taunted her, the more determined she became not to respond. For Trina's
sake, she became as sweet and self-effacing as she
could be, at least on the surface.

Instead of appeasing him, however, her com-
pliance only made him angrier, until he slapped a
lens cover over his camera and snapped, 'Take a
break. I need it, even if you don't.'

While Rowan stamped off into a corner and stood
looking moodily out at the view, Tony thrust a
paper cup of steaming coffee into her hands. 'You
look as if you could use this,' he murmured
sympathetically.

She sipped it gratefully. 'Thanks. Is he always as difficult as this?'

Tony shrugged. 'You'd know the answer to that better than me.'

As she perched on a stool to sip her coffee, Tony watched her appraisingly. What had she said wrong? Maybe Trina knew Rowan Traynor and his assistant better than she had admitted. She tensed as Tony started towards her. 'Trina...?'

His progress was arrested by the studio door swinging open. A tall, solidly built man in a business suit stepped in, and Tony swerved to greet him. 'Mr Andrews. This is a pleasant surprise.'

'Just keeping an eye on the budget,' the man responded. 'Traynor has a reputation for demanding the best, and never mind who has to pay for it.'

'If you want rubbish, there are plenty of other photographers you can go to,' Rowan said smoothly, making no move to shake the man's hand. He slid a hand under Danni's arm and propelled her forward. 'Lyle Andrews—I don't think you've met your model, Trina Dare.'

This man must be the client who was paying for this morning's activity, she guessed as the man's eyes swept her from head to toe, his lips parting into a lascivious smile. 'Miss Dare—may I call you Trina? Trina, you were made for my company's designs.'

She didn't like the way he was undressing her with his eyes, even though she had responded quite differently when Rowan had done much the same thing. There was no respect in Lyle Andrews' expression, only a calculating shrewdness which made her think he was putting a price on her head. 'Thank you,' she said, inclining her head.

'Mind if I sit in for a while?' Mr Andrews asked, settling himself in one of the canvas-backed chairs before anyone could object.

'Suit yourself,' Rowan said, turning back to his camera. Over his shoulder, he said, 'I'd like the see-through number next, Trina.'

Oh, he would, would he? It was as if, seeing the way his client had eyed her so frankly, he had deliberately picked a provocative swimsuit to provoke *her*. Her eyes flashed fire, but she lifted her chin determinedly. If Trina could carry this off, then so would she, but inwardly she damned him to hell for treating her like this.

The suit was downright indecent, made of sheer black chiffon with tiny, black leather stars covering her nipples, and a tiny triangle of leather purporting to be the bottom half. It would have looked at home on the stage of a nightclub in King's Cross!

She was aware of the client's eyes following her as she crossed the room to the cyclorama. Then he purpled. 'Hang on! That isn't part of our range. The overseas buyers would have a fit if we included anything as daring as that. I'll admit it looks fantastic on you, Trina, but it won't do at all.'

'Sorry, my mistake,' Rowan murmured evenly, not looking at her. 'We'd better have the crocheted bikini then, darling.'

He did that on purpose, she fumed as she re-
treated to her corner to change. He must have
slipped the black see-through number on to the rack
while she was having her coffee, making her put it
on in front of the client to humiliate her. What sort
of game was he playing with her...? With Trina,
she corrected herself mentally.

By the time they broke for lunch, her nerves were
in shreds, and she wasn't sure how much more of
Rowan's sarcasm she could stand. If she only had
a telephone number where she could contact Trina,
she could find out what had been going on between
Rowan and her twin. There had to be some logical
explanation for his outrageous behaviour towards
her/Trina.

But there was worse to come.

As she stepped off the cyclorama after the last
shot of the morning, Lyle Andrews stood up,
moving uncomfortably close to her. 'I'd like to buy
you some lunch, my dear,' he said softly, but not
so softly that Rowan didn't catch the invitation.
She saw him watching her speculatively.

She bit her lip. What would Trina say to such an
invitation? No! This was definitely above and
beyond the call of duty. 'I'm sorry, I can't be away
too long, we still have a lot more to do,' she said,
smiling sweetly, while shuddering inwardly at the
man.

Rowan stretched luxuriously. 'That's all right,
Trina. You run along with Mr Andrews. I want to

process this morning's film, so you can take as long as you like.'

Her heart sank. She had a fair idea where lunch with a man like Andrews was expected to lead. 'Oh, no, I couldn't,' she protested.

Rowan's lips tightened into an implacable line. 'Of course you can. Tell you what, Lyle, you can have the use of my penthouse for a couple of hours.'

He tossed a bunch of keys to Lyle, and the man's eyes positively gleamed. 'That's very decent of you,' he said, running his tongue over his thin lips.

She had the feeling she had been outmanoeuvred, and she couldn't for the life of her see any way out, without admitting who she really was. In moody silence, she changed into her street clothes, but Rowan followed her and leaned idly across the corner, effectively blocking any escape with one casually placed arm. 'I'm glad you agreed to have lunch with the client,' he drawled.

'You seem to have done most of the agreeing,' she hissed back. 'You can see what he wants for lunch—me!'

He shrugged. 'So what? That's the way things are done in this business—as you should know.'

Was she imagining it, or was there a shade too much emphasis in that last phrase? In truth, she *didn't* know, but couldn't say so now without betraying Trina and jeopardising her twin's career. 'I understand,' she said resignedly, mentally preparing herself to fight for her honour at Rowan's penthouse.

As she went out of the studio door with Lyle Andrews trying unsuccessfully to catch her arm, Rowan winked at her. 'Have a good lunch, Trina—you've earned it!'

CHAPTER THREE

THEY accomplished the drive to Rowan's apartment block in silence—hers stony and impassive, Lyle Andrews' clearly anticipatory. 'It was good of Traynor to let us lunch at his place,' he said into the silence.

She kept her face deadpan. 'Yes. He's all heart.'

Rowan lived in a block which was clearly expensive, betrayed by the classic proportions of the architect-designed building, and emphasised by the obsequiousness of the doorman who showed them to the lift. 'Does himself proud,' Lyle observed as they rode up to the penthouse floor. It was obvious that he thought Rowan did so at his company's expense.

When they let themselves in, Danni gave an involuntary gasp of admiration. The penthouse was on three levels and was decorated almost entirely in creamy beige, the simplicity of the scheme creating an air of light and spaciousness. To the left of the main entrance, a spiral staircase led to the upper floors, and the open planning revealed a series of skylights let into the highest level, flooding the whole place with brilliant natural light.

The first level was taken up largely by a ballroom-sized living-room, with windows opening on to a fabulous view of the North Sydney skyline. It was a cool, elegant room, sparsely furnished with sofas arranged in conversation groups. A glass and chrome bar took up half of one wall, and behind it were hung framed photographs, which Danni assumed to be Rowan's own work.

'Let's take a look at the other floors,' Lyle said eagerly, plainly pleased with having her all to himself in such a sumptuous setting.

'Can't we stay here and admire the view?' she asked lamely.

'That isn't what we came for,' he reminded her coolly, taking her arm and steering her towards the spiral staircase. His grip on her arm was biting, and she could see she was going to have trouble fending him off when the time came.

The second level was a mezzanine overlooking the lounge, the dining area defined by open mesh painted the same cool beige as the walls. A galley kitchen opened off it on the right, and on the left Danni found herself looking through the open door of a master bedroom.

Lyle followed her gaze to the big circular bed taking up most of the room. It boasted the only touch of colour in the apartment so far—a Marimekko bedspread subtly patterned in unconventional pink. 'We'll check out that room later,' he said boldly. 'Right now, you'd better see to our lunch. Rowan said I could help myself to anything I found here.'

Did that include her? she wondered, her skin starting to prickle. Rowan must have a serious dislike for her twin to expose her to such a flagrant wolf as Lyle Andrews, even providing the setting for him to indulge his whims. Unless, of course, that was how Rowan himself got his kicks. She shuddered at the thought. She should never have started this crazy escapade.

But it was too late to go back now. She took a hesitant step towards the kitchen. 'I'll ... I'll see what there is for lunch.' Maybe, while she was preparing some food, she could figure out some way of escape.

'Ah, there you are. Mr Traynor rang and told me to expect you for lunch.' Both Danni and Lyle stared in astonishment as a tall, thin woman emerged from the kitchen. She was smartly dressed in a green linen shirtwaister with a frilled apron over the top. 'I'm Dora Howard, Mr Traynor's housekeeper,' she said to Lyle, then smiled at Danni. 'It's lovely to see you again, my dear.'

Seeing Lyle's jaw drop open, Danni wanted to laugh aloud with relief. With the housekeeper here to chaperon her, there was no way Lyle could get up to anything. 'I'm so happy you're here, Mrs Howard,' she said, heartfelt, not looking at Lyle.

'Are you sure Traynor didn't say you could take the afternoon off?' he asked churlishly.

Her eyes widened. 'Goodness, no! I have lunch all prepared, and Mr Traynor specially asked me to stick around in case there was anything else I can do for you.'

'As the lady said, he's all heart,' Lyle muttered under his breath.

Only as they sat down at the table did reaction begin to set in, and Danni felt a shudder pass through her. Rowan had deliberately let her think he was pairing her off with Lyle Andrews, knowing she was in no position to do anything about it. Trina or no Trina, she was going to give him a piece of her mind when she got back to the studio. How dared he set her up like this?

Lunch was a triumph for Danni, and an obvious let-down for Lyle. Every time he leaned across to pat her hand, it seemed as if Dora Howard was hovering over them, asking if there was anything else they wanted.

'Nothing you can provide,' Lyle muttered after one such request.

Mrs Howard sniffed loudly, indicating that she had heard. 'I'll bring the coffee,' she said stiffly.

It was all Danni could do not to collapse into helpless giggles when Lyle scraped his chair back and stood up. 'I'm going back to the office.'

Danni smiled innocently. 'Thanks for the lunch invitation, Mr Andrews. We must do this again some time.'

He threw a look of disgust towards the kitchen. 'I'm not all that keen on threesomes.'

With a curt word of farewell he left, slamming the door behind him. Danni waited until she was sure he had gone, then gave in to the laughter which had been welling up inside her throughout lunch.

'What's so funny?' Mrs Howard asked, setting a cup of coffee in front of her.

Danni wiped her eyes with the back of her hand. 'It's all right. I was picturing Lyle Andrews' face when he walked in here and saw you. You'd better have his coffee, by the way. He had to go back to the office.'

'I can imagine. Fancy him thinking Mr Traynor would let you come here alone with a man like that!'

Since it was precisely what Danni thought he had done, she sobered at once. 'I suppose not,' she said quietly, then rose smoothly. 'I'd better be getting back to the studio myself. Thanks for the lunch, Mrs Howard.'

The housekeeper forestalled her. 'I was coming to tell you—Mr Traynor rang and asked if you would wait here for him. He said he wants to talk to you.'

Oh, he did, did he? Well, she was just as keen to talk to him, although upbraid was a better word than talk. But she wasn't going to let herself in for any more misunderstandings. Once a day was quite enough. 'Will you give him my apologies? I'm afraid I can't wait.'

'He'll be disappointed,' Mrs Howard warned her.

He'll get over it, she thought sourly, but the housekeeper had been too kind for her to voice her thought, so she smiled gently. 'I'm sorry, but I have an appointment later on. I'm sure Mr Traynor will understand.'

Mrs Howard looked doubtful. 'I don't know ... but I suppose I can't make you stay if you don't want to.'

Evidently, the housekeeper was accustomed to treating Rowan Traynor's word as law, and expected everyone else to do the same. What a tyrant he must be in his home! 'When I see him, I'll make sure he knows you delivered his message, and that it was my own decision not to stay.' There, that should keep the housekeeper out of trouble with her boss.

But Mrs Howard didn't seem any happier. 'As you wish,' she murmured. 'Can I tell him you'll at least telephone him?'

'Oh, yes, you can tell him that.' No need to add that it wouldn't be until tomorrow morning when she rang him for a weather check, to ensure that the weather was suitable for the location shots. Trina had briefed her on this bit of protocol.

'Good, I'll tell him to expect your call,' Mrs Howard said, her expression relieved.

Feeling much happier than when she had arrived, Danni let herself out of the sumptuous apartment. With a sense of satisfaction, she pictured Rowan Traynor sitting by the telephone this evening, waiting for her to call. Serve him right for setting her up with Lyle Andrews this afternoon!

Briefly, she wondered what he wanted to talk to her about. Work, most likely, or perhaps it was the strange situation which evidently existed between him and her twin. Why else would he be treating her so callously—unless he had something against her sister? It was plain that Trina hadn't told her anything about the relationship between herself and Rowan.

Preoccupied with the puzzle, she rode down to the ground floor and was shown out by the doorman.

If she had been more alert, she might not have been caught unawares when a large, maroon-coloured car slid to a stop beside her and a door opened. Before she could react, she was taken by the arm and urged towards the car.

'Let me go!' she began to scream, the sound dying in her throat as she recognised Lyle Andrews. 'You!'

'Yes, me,' he said nastily, his smile reminding her of a crocodile she'd seen at Taronga Zoo. 'Traynor thought he was being cute, but I can be just as clever. Get in.'

She clung to the door of the car. This was like a nightmare! How could he get away with this in broad daylight, in the middle of the city?

As she resisted, he tugged harder. 'Come on, darling, you know you want to. I could make it well worth your while.'

The suggestion that she might actually be willing to accompany such a sleazy character was the final straw. With a mighty effort, she pulled free of him and flung herself backwards, against the wall of Rowan's apartment building. For a moment, she thought that Andrews might be going to get out of the car, then he seemed to think better of it. As she cowered against the wall, he reached for the passenger-door. 'I can see I was wrong about you, sweetheart. You aren't worth the trouble.'

'What the hell's going on here?'

Danni's head jerked back, and relief flooded through her as she saw Rowan striding towards them. Acting on instinct, she ran to his side and his arm closed protectively around her.

The fury in Rowan's voice had scared Andrews. He kept his hand on the door as he looked up into Rowan's stormy face. 'This was your idea, remember?'

Rowan's expression was contemptuous. 'You don't need any help to come up with your ideas. Get out of here.'

Needing no more encouragement, Andrews slammed the door, flung the car into gear and took off with a screech of tyre-rubber. Watching him go, Danni sagged against Rowan. 'I'm glad you showed up. He was trying to "persuade" me to get into his car.'

'What were you doing out here, anyway?' Rowan demanded. 'Dora Howard was supposed to be keeping an eye on you.'

'She was, but I . . . I decided to go home. Now I wish I'd waited as you asked me to.'

He fixed her with a dubious look. 'There's a first time for everything, I suppose.'

Shock made her respond more sharply than she intended. 'It's all very well for you to criticise me, but you were the one who suggested I come out with that creep in the first place.'

He nodded grimly. 'I should have known better. I can only say I'm sorry, and ask you to believe I didn't intend things to work out this way.'

'I know you didn't,' she conceded. If she really had been Trina, she would probably have understood what was behind this. As it was, she was confused and exhausted after the strain of the day's events.

He read the exhaustion on her face. 'You need a drink. Come back up with me and have one, then I'll drive you home. I think it's time we talked.'

Fresh panic assailed her. What could they talk about without revealing her true identity? And how could he possibly drive her to Trina's address? The minute she directed him to her own flat, he would know she was an impostor.

Refusing his offer would only make him suspicious, so she had little choice but to let him escort her upstairs. Dora Howard seemed surprised to see her again, but tactfully said nothing and went off to make the drinks Rowan ordered.

Danni sat tensely on the edge of a sofa. She still felt shaken by her encounter with Lyle Andrews. What an awful man he was. 'Why do you put up with him as a client?' she asked Rowan.

Distaste coloured his expression. 'I don't. A very good friend of mine is the real client. He has the misfortune to have Andrews as a brother-in-law, so he can't even fire him. But I can. First thing tomorrow, I'll make sure he's taken off the swimwear account.'

Danni felt relieved that the man wouldn't be on the scene any more, but she was puzzled as to why Rowan had put Trina in such a difficult position to begin with. Again, she wished her twin had been more forthright.

The silence between them stretched into minutes, while she perched on the edge of the couch, frantically trying to think of an excuse to leave before she betrayed either herself or Trina. Here in his home, Rowan was so obviously the master, at ease, and yet she was aware of a sense of tightly leashed power which made her feel as if she was caged with a tiger. He stood up, and his physical presence became even more overwhelming. Automatically, she stood up, rather than be at such a disadvantage to him, then almost immediately wished she hadn't when her move brought her alongside him, so his warm breath fanned her burning cheeks. 'What is it?' she asked as he loomed over her.

'There's something I've been wanting to do, but we always seem to have an audience,' he growled.

'For what?' she asked, trying unsuccessfully to control the tremor which rippled through her voice. What could he have in mind?

She soon found out when he took her in his arms, his hold possessive and irresistible. Then his mouth claimed hers in a kiss which was giving and demanding by turns.

She had been kissed before, but never by anyone as charismatic as Rowan. As his hand cupped the back of her head and his mouth moulded over hers, she thought dizzily of burgundy wine, dark chocolate and rare spices. He evoked memories of every exotic taste she had ever experienced, all combined with an indefinable maleness which bombarded her senses almost to the point of overload.

It was a shock when Rowan released her mouth and looked at her, his expression distracted. 'I shouldn't have done that.'

'Why not?' For her, it had felt bewilderingly right.

'Because, damn it, I'm not in the habit of kissing impostors!'

It took her a moment to register what he had just said, then her eyes widened with shock. 'You know?'

He nodded, and she felt hot waves of anger surging over her. He had known and had still taken advantage of his knowledge to kiss her! The wonder of his kiss drained away, leaving her feeling used and cheap. 'How long have you known?'

'I admit I was fooled the day you walked into Monarch Magazines, but then I was too tired to put two and two together. I knew the truth as soon as I walked into my studio and found you cowering behind the screen like a scared kid. No real model acts like that. You had to be a ring-in.'

'Yet you didn't say anything. You let me go right on making a fool of myself.'

He shook his head. 'No more of a fool than you were trying to make of me. I wanted to see just how far you would go with your charade.'

It was becoming clear to her now. 'You made me wear that see-through swimsuit and sent me to lunch with Lyle Andrews, knowing that I couldn't refuse without revealing who I was.'

'That was more or less the idea,' he agreed.

A chill shook her. 'How could you be so callous? I ended up having to fight Andrews off when he wanted to get me into his car.'

Cynical amusement glinted in his eyes. He seemed oblivious to her anger, which was building in the face of his subtle mockery. 'I knew Dora would look after you. If you'd done as I asked and stayed here with her, you would have been quite safe.'

'But I didn't know that, did I? Of all the ego-tistical, self-opinionated men...' She was unaware that she had formed the intention to lash out until her hand flew towards his face.

He caught her wrist before she could land the blow. Twist as she liked, she was powerless to free

herself from his iron grasp. 'Now, just a minute—
you were the one who was trying to deceive me.
You deserved all you got. All you had to do was
confess, and I would never have let you come here
with Andrews. You were the one keeping the
charade going, not me, so you have no one to blame
but yourself if your joke has backfired.'

He was right, and her fury subsided as she realised it. 'All right, I'm sorry. I was wrong to
pretend that I was Trina, but it wasn't a joke,
honestly.'

His grip on her arm eased slightly. 'Well, at least
we agree on something. Now, suppose you sit down
and tell me just what's going on.'

CHAPTER FOUR

DANNI was given a few moments' respite when Dora Howard returned with their drinks. Unobtrusively, she set them down on a table, then vanished in the direction of the kitchen. Danni watched her go with a feeling of despair. She had been hoping Rowan's housekeeper would stay around, saving her from beginning her explanation. Her stomach churned at the prospect, and she found herself hoping that Rowan wouldn't think too badly of her once he knew the whole story.

Her hopes of a sympathetic hearing were soon dashed. He leaned across the table and picked up his drink, sipping it before he fixed her with a gimlet stare. 'All right, let's start with your real name.'

'I'm Danielle O'Dare, Trina's sister,' she said in a subdued voice.

Rowan nodded, as if she was only confirming what he had already suspected. 'Ages ago, Trina told me she had a twin, but she gave me the impression that she was joking. Obviously, she wasn't.'

'It wouldn't be much of a joke, would it?' Danni said miserably.

The first glimmer of softness seeped into his steely-blue gaze, causing her spirits to lift slightly. 'No, it wouldn't. Do you two make a habit of changing places?'

'Of course not!' she shot back angrily. 'Usually we keep our professional lives a long way apart.'

'But not this time,' he observed, staring moodily into his drink before returning his gaze to her. 'Tell me, to what do I owe this honour?'

His sarcasm stung her like a lash. Since she had been trying to do him a favour by stepping into Trina's shoes, it was unfair of him to be so unforgiving before he had heard her out. She reached for her handbag and stood up. 'I can see you've already made up your mind about me, so there's no point in further post mortems, is there?'

Before she could move away, his fingers closed around her wrist. 'Sit down, and stop being childish.'

'I'm not,' she protested, but he drew her implacably down until she was once more seated opposite him. 'Are you always so cruel?'

'Only when it's called for,' was his curt response. 'Now, where were we?'

She blinked back the angry tears which sprang to her eyes. 'You were being needlessly sarcastic,' she reminded him coldly. 'I was trying to tell you my story.'

He folded his arms. 'I'm still waiting.'

How could she have thought such a cold, unfeeling man was attractive? No wonder Trina hadn't wanted to work with him! Since he wasn't going to let her leave until he'd had his pound of flesh, she decided to get it over as quickly as possible.

'Trina was too ill to handle your assignment this week,' she plunged in. 'She needed to rest, so I agreed to take over rather than let her clients down.'

'That was big of her,' he murmured drily, sounding as if he didn't think so for a minute. 'I wonder if she expected you to take over *all* of her responsibilities.'

Danni regarded him warily. 'What do you mean?'

'Trina and I had been seeing each other outside working hours.'

This was a complication she hadn't foreseen. 'She didn't tell me,' she confessed weakly.

'I gathered as much.'

To give her shaking hands something to do, she picked up her drink and touched the cold glass to her lips, but her throat was too tight to swallow anything and she set it down again. 'How well did you know my sister?'

'Well enough to be sure what caused her sudden spate of ill health.' Danni waited, sure there was more, and he went on. 'I wanted more from a relationship than she was willing or able to give. She wanted me to be one of her crowd of admirers. I finally told her I was a one-woman man, and I expected her to be a one-man woman, which resulted in a blazing row and she walked out. Hence her reluctance to come and work with me this week.'

Tracing patterns on the sofa with her fingernail, Danni said softly, 'I see.' Why hadn't Trina told her any of this, instead of pretending to be ill? Because, had she been honest, Danni would never have agreed to take over for her, an inner voice replied. Trina had used the one means of persuasion against which Danni had no defence—her fragile health. She felt a surge of anger at Trina for getting her into this mess.

Rowan broke into her thoughts. 'You hadn't a clue what you were getting into, had you?'

'No. I really believed she was ill.'

His mouth tightened fractionally. 'Are you always so quick to come to her rescue?'

She shook her head, then felt he was entitled to more than just the bare bones of the story, so she explained how Trina had saved her life in their teens. 'So you see, I owe her more than I can ever repay,' she concluded.

'And, knowing Trina, she will make sure you never forget it,' he observed.

Although her first instinct was to fly to her twin's defence, she kept silent, knowing that he was right. Trina had taken advantage of Danni's debt too often for argument on this point. Despite telling herself that each time would be the last, Danni still found herself giving in. That it might not always be in Trina's best interests she was now forced to acknowledge.

'For what it's worth, I am sorry that I tried to deceive you,' she said whole-heartedly.

He appraised her slowly, the penetrating blue of his gaze making her feel as if he could see to the depths of her soul. 'Yes, I believe you are,' he said at last.

Relief and gladness swept over her. He believed her! She shouldn't care what he thought, but the discovery made her feel light-headed. How could Trina look at another man when Rowan was around? she found herself thinking, then caught herself in annoyance. He had already shown her that he could be hard and unrelenting. She would be foolish to misread his compassionate gaze as anything more, whatever the temptation.

It occurred to her that Trina's attitude must have hurt him badly. Danni knew better than anyone what a flirt her sister could be. It was something they could never agree about. Danni herself was what Rowan had called a one-man woman. If that man satisfied her, she could see no reason to look further. Trina, however, had needed the re-assurance of a crowd of admirers since their schooldays. It didn't surprise Danni that Trina was still the same. What *did* surprise her was finding that a man as powerfully masculine as Rowan Traynor still wasn't enough to satisfy Trina's thirst for male admiration.

Watching as he cradled his glass in long, elegantly tapering fingers, she recalled how those same fingers had felt brushing the soft skin of her back and shoulders as he helped her to dress in the studio. Her mouth still felt swollen and bruised from his kiss, and she touched the back of her hand to her mouth dreamily. Realising what she was doing, she dropped her hand quickly, upsetting the drink on the table beside her. Hearing the crash, Dora Howard hurried in and mopped up the spill, dismissing Danni's effusive apologies. The brief drama gave Danni the respite she needed to regain her composure.

How could she be thinking of Rowan Traynor in any romantic way? she asked herself in annoyance. She made herself remember that he had only kissed her to provoke her into admitting who she really was. And he had just explained that it was Trina

who had left him, not the other way around. There
was no point in Danni indulging in fantasies about
him until she knew how he felt about her twin.

She had learned at least that much in her twenty-
five years. Her experience with Keith Bowden
should have been enough of a lesson, without her
making the same mistake over Rowan. Keith was
a tall, bronzed surf life-saver who had captured
Danni's heart, convincing her that he was the love
of her life. She had begun to dream of marriage to
him, until he had begun cancelling their dates, and
she found out he was seeing Trina instead. When
Danni had confronted him, he'd admitted that he'd
only been dating her in order to get to know Trina.
Whatever attacks of conscience Trina might have
felt over appropriating Danni's man had been out-
weighed by Trina's need for male attention. The
atmosphere between the sisters had been strained,
until Danni had realised that Trina would never see
what she had done wrong, and made it up with her.

By unspoken agreement they had kept their love-
lives separated since then, not even meeting each
other's dates, which was why Danni hadn't known
about Rowan until now.

Watching Rowan as he prowled around his
apartment, she was saddened to think that she
wouldn't see him again after this. But the game was
over. It was time she resumed her own identity and
her own life. She picked up her bag and stood up.
'I'm glad we got everything straightened out,
Rowan. I suppose this is goodbye?'

His eyebrows arched as he swung back to her. 'What are you talking about? You can't just walk out now, you have a job to do.'

'*Trina* has a job to do,' she reminded him, trying not to let him see how much she wished things were different. 'I'm a journalist by profession, not a model,' she added.

He made a show of looking around the room. 'I don't see Trina around here anywhere, do you?'

Now he was the one being childish. 'Of course I don't. She went away for a few days to have a rest.'

'I don't suppose she told you where you could contact her?'

'No, she didn't,' she conceded reluctantly. Until he mentioned it, she hadn't really thought it odd that Trina hadn't left her any means of getting in touch. What would have happened if Danni had needed her help with the modelling job?

Rowan watched the play of emotions across her face. 'I thought as much. So it means you're stuck with the job.'

'But I can't be! You said yourself that I was wooden and terrible.' Her voice was vibrant with distress.

'Not terrible, just inexperienced. Actually, you weren't doing as badly as I tried to make out. I just wanted to goad you into confessing you were an impostor.'

Even as she realised he was paying her a compliment, she shook her head. 'The answer is still no.'

He frowned. 'I'm afraid I can't accept that.'

She stared at him in astonishment. 'You can't accept it? You don't have any choice.'

'Neither do you, Danielle. I have to get this catalogue finished on deadline. As a journalist, you know what a deadline means?' She nodded impassively, still stunned into silence. 'Without Trina, you're the only model I've got. You started this, so I think you ought to finish it.'

In the face of his persistence, some of her feelings of insecurity vanished. He sounded as if he really wanted to work with her. All the same, she wished he wouldn't try to force her to stay. She couldn't help asking, 'What if I don't agree?'

His response caught her by surprise. 'How easily do you think you'd get a reporting job if I started a rumour that it really was you in the centrefold spread?'

Remembering Mrs Philmont's reaction, she knew what would happen. 'That's a low threat!' she fumed. 'Nobody would believe you.'

'I'm prepared to take the risk,' he said easily. 'What about you?'

She couldn't and he knew it. The newspaper world thrived on rumours. If word got around that she modelled nude in her spare time, she'd never live it down. Her reputation as a serious writer would be in shreds. It was a high price, but she knew there was only one answer to such a threat. 'I'd have to risk it,' she said heavily. 'If I gave in to pressure like that, I'd have no career left, anyway.' She let him digest this in silence for a few minutes before adding, 'But I'll finish the assignment if you ask me nicely.'

His blue eyes flashed fire as he regarded her with grudging admiration. 'Ye gods, you are different from Trina, aren't you?' He dragged his fingers through his hair, tousling it. 'Very well, Danielle, I'm asking you nicely to come and work for me again.'

'In that case, I accept.'

His breath whistled out between clenched teeth. 'I'm glad we got that settled. Are you always such a tough negotiator?'

She smiled, relaxing for the first time that day. 'I don't mean to be tough. I just have these old-fashioned things called principles.'

He drained his glass with a flourish. 'Maybe that's why I failed to recognise them. Principles aren't all that common in this business.'

'Or in most businesses nowadays,' she agreed.

His answering smile was so luminous that she almost looked to see if a light had been turned on in the room. She leaned forward, unconsciously basking in the glow of his powerful personality. When he turned his charm on full-bore like this, it was difficult to recall why on earth she had considered not working with him. Careful, girl, she cautioned herself. He was a business associate, nothing more.

His next words reminded her of this even more forcibly. 'I'll try to keep the assignment as short as possible from here on.'

Had she misread his keenness to work with her? 'Is there a time problem?' she asked, feeling cold suddenly.

'I should remember that modelling isn't your real business,' he explained. 'It wouldn't be fair of me to monopolise your time.' Before she could insist that she didn't mind, he went on, half to himself, 'In fact, if we can get Trina to finish the assignment, you'd be off the hook altogether.'

She swallowed her disappointment. So he would still rather work with Trina if it could be arranged. 'How do you plan to get in touch with her?' she asked with difficulty.

'I don't know yet. There's one chance, but it's a long shot. But I can't do anything in time for tomorrow's shoot at Bondi Beach. Do you mind going on with this for one more day?'

She would go on with it for much longer, but it seemed as if Rowan didn't want her to. It could be out of consideration for Danni, as he said, but it was more likely because he preferred to spend the time with Trina. In Danni's experience, men had always preferred her twin's company but, somehow, she had expected Rowan to be the exception. Was it because she enjoyed his company so much? Thinking this way was a waste, since Rowan had evidently made his choice, so Danni stood up. 'I'd better be going. Thanks for the drink.'

She refused his offer of a lift home, insisting that she had errands to do on the way. But he stayed in her thoughts all the way home, dominating her evening and even intruding on her dreams. Despite all the reasons why she shouldn't be looking forward to it, she found she could hardly wait to get to Bondi Beach next morning.

*   *   *

Since it was the middle of the week, she could have driven to the beach and been assured of a parking space, but she decided not to chance it and caught a taxi to Bondi instead.

Rowan's Mercedes sports car was parked alongside a red Ford Transit van, which she guessed belonged to Tony. The assistant popped his head out of the door in answer to her knock. 'All the garments are in here, so you can use the van to change in,' he explained as he jumped down beside her.

The first swimsuit she was to model was a diagonally striped *maillot* cut away at each side, so it was more like a bikini linked by a ribbon of fabric at back and front. Wearing it, she climbed out of the van. Rowan and Tony were setting up their equipment at the southern end of the vast crescent of sand, disturbingly close to the area reserved for topless sunbathers. She was suddenly glad that Rowan knew she wasn't Trina. At least he wouldn't expect her to pose topless.

But after photographing the *maillot* against the colourful backdrop of the esplanade and the pavilion, he came up to her and started to slide the straps off her shoulders. She shrugged away his hands. 'What are you doing?'

'Don't worry, this is the topless area. You won't get arrested,' he assured her.

She felt herself flooding with colour which had nothing to do with the sun's heat. 'I don't care. These aren't supposed to be semi-nude shots.'

'I know, these are for my private collection,' he explained, adding, 'Trina wouldn't mind doing them like this.'

'But I'm not Trina, am I?' Angrily, she stepped back, away from his outstretched hand and straight into a hole washed out by the tide. She gave a cry of dismay as she felt herself tumbling backwards.

Before she could sprawl all her length on the sand, Rowan's arms closed around her and she was pulled against his hard, muscular body. The sudden contact knocked the breath out of her, and she clutched at Rowan. He held her against him longer than was strictly necessary and, to her surprise, she found she welcomed his touch, which was strong and secure. Her scanty costume made her conscious of every contour of his virile body. A shock-wave travelled through her, which she unwillingly recognised as desire for him.

She made a feeble attempt to free herself. 'Thanks for catching me. I'm sorry, I'm not usually so clumsy.'

Although he released her, his compelling gaze held her in thrall. 'I'm the one who should apologise. I guess you look so much like Trina that I can't believe you don't behave like her.'

'Well, now you know,' she said huskily, trying without success to blame her shortness of breath on her near fall. It couldn't have anything to do with the intent way he was looking at her.

She wanted to ask him whether he was pleased or disappointed because she was so different from Trina, but she bit back the question, finding that she was afraid of his answer. 'I'd better change into the next costume,' she said, deliberately changing the subject. 'Otherwise we'll be here all day and night.'

'Not tonight,' he said, sounding distracted. 'I meant to tell you about that. There's a media preview of my new photographic exhibition this evening. Would you like to come?'

The tightness in her chest relaxed slightly; he wanted her to go out with him tonight! 'I'd love to,' she said enthusiastically.

'Good, because I have a feeling your twin might show up there tonight.'

Was that the only reason he wanted her to be there? 'What makes you think she'll come?' she forced herself to ask, veiling her disappointment.

'I arranged for an influential fashion editor to send her an invitation, knowing she couldn't turn this particular lady down.' He inspected her face, which she knew reflected her disenchantment. 'You seem upset. I thought you'd be pleased to be getting out of this job.'

She shrugged. 'I suppose so.' Now that Rowan knew she wasn't a clone of her sister, it seemed he was keen to end their association. 'What will you do if Trina doesn't show up?' she asked.

His shoulders sloped in an expressive gesture. 'We'll cross that bridge when we come to it, shall we?'

For the remainder of the day, as Danni posed for him, she was achingly aware that it could be for the last time. Once Trina returned to work, there would be no place for Danni here. It was probably just as well, she told herself. She had had enough of being a stand-in for Trina where men were concerned.

All the same, as she got ready to go to Rowan's exhibition that evening, she found herself hoping that Trina wouldn't show up.

CHAPTER FIVE

IN CONTRAST to his fashion work, Rowan's exhibition was of dramatic black and white portraits, some of famous people, but others showing individuals going about their daily lives. Danni stood for a long time in front of a picture of an old woman feeding pigeons in Centennial Park.

'Like it?' Rowan asked, coming up behind her.

'It says something about how life goes on,' she observed without turning round. 'There's the woman at the end of her life, nurturing the birds, with the little girl watching her, representing the next generation.'

She half expected him to scoff at her attempt to express what the picture meant to her, but he touched her shoulder in a gesture of companionship. 'I'm glad you get so much out of it. I try to make some kind of statement with all my pictures.'

'The Kampuchean ones are quite chilling. You're against war, aren't you?' This time she did turn round, surprising a look of sadness on his finely chiselled features.

'I'm against destruction,' he amended. 'We spend too much time tearing things down, instead of building them up, feeding the hungry and housing the homeless. Sorry, I don't mean to sound like I'm rehearsing for the TV cameras.'

She had seen the news crew arriving at the same time as herself and Rowan, but she didn't think his views were just for the record. They sounded too honestly held. No matter what Rowan's reasons for inviting her here, she was glad she had come. Seeing what he called his serious work gave her an insight into his character which was startlingly different from the image he projected in his commercial activities.

He touched her arm. 'Will you be all right for a while? The TV people are signalling me for their interview.'

'I know quite a few people here, so I'll be fine,' she assured him, and he went to join the waiting crew, stepping into the dazzling circle of lights like a boxer entering the ring.

She watched him for a few minutes, then continued her inspection of the photographs. It was true, she did know many of the journalists and photographers who were here for the preview, but she didn't feel like talking shop right now. Only one person had so far mistaken her for Trina, and that was the fashion editor who had invited Trina to come.

At first, the editor had accused her of playing a joke when she introduced herself. It was only when Danni showed her a photograph of her and Trina that the editor was finally convinced. 'It's amazing,' she mouthed, inspecting the picture. 'Now, if they could only get the two of you to do a centrefold together, the issue would be a sell-out!'

She drifted away before Danni could react to such an idea. It *would* be a sell-out, she conceded, but on her part, not the magazine's.

Resting against a stone pillar, she surveyed the crowd, nodding to the people who waved greetings to her. Suddenly, she straightened as she caught sight of Trina coming into the room on the arm of a tall, sandy-haired man in his early forties. Trina saw her at the same moment and tugged at her companion's arm, as if trying to urge him to leave. He said something to Trina and they continued into the room. Desperately, Danni pushed her way through the crowd to her twin's side.

'I suppose the line is, fancy meeting you here,' Trina said with forced brightness.

'Rowan thought you might show up,' Danni replied.

Trina's expression became alarmed. 'Rowan? But he never comes to his own showings.'

'Well, he did this time, and he wants to talk to you.'

The man at Trina's side turned from greeting someone, and looked stunned as he caught sight of Danni. 'Good grief, there's two of you, Trina, and I haven't even had a drink yet,' he said in a strong American accent.

Trina took his arm. 'It's all right, Mal. Malcolm Sutton, this is my twin sister, Danielle. I told you I had a twin, remember?'

Malcolm's eyes were fixed on Danni. 'You didn't say she was your mirror image.'

Danni held out her hand. 'I'm pleased to meet you, Malcolm.'

With an effort, Malcolm stirred from his trance and shook her hand. 'Delighted, Danielle. Did I hear you saying that Rowan Traynor was here? He's a brilliant photographer. I'd like to meet him.'

'But first a drink for the dynamic duo,' Trina said, urging Malcolm in the direction of the bar, which was barely visible for the crowd around it.

'Yes, of course. Champagne for you both?' They nodded, and he moved towards the bar.

Trina watched him go, then leaned towards Danni. 'Watch what you say about Rowan in front of Malcolm. I just might marry him.'

Masking her surprise, Danni pulled her twin into an empty office and closed the door, muting the noise from the gallery. 'Never mind Malcolm. I want to know what's going on with you and Rowan.'

Trina's flushed expression gave her away even as she said, 'I don't know what you mean.'

'Oh, no? Why didn't you tell me you were not only working for Rowan, you were dating him as well?'

'You didn't ask.'

The lateness of the hour and the strain of the day did nothing for Danni's temper. 'Really, Trina! You know you had a fight with Rowan and couldn't face working with him, so you let me stand in for you.'

'It wasn't as bad as that,' Trina denied, then fixed Danni with a sharp look. 'From the way you're reacting, anyone would think you fancied him yourself.'

'Don't be ridiculous!' Danni snapped back, although she was uncomfortably aware that it was true. 'After Keith Bowden, I promised never to get involved with any man of yours, remember?'

'Don't tell me you're still harping on Keith. I didn't know how you felt about him, did I?'

'That's not the point,' Danni said tiredly, aware that Trina was doing her usual trick of changing the subject. 'The point is, you and Rowan apparently have some unfinished business.'

'It's finished as far as I'm concerned,' Trina said huffily. 'Rowan was interested in me, but he wasn't prepared to take me as I am.'

'You mean he wasn't thrilled about you seeing other men?' Danni amended, and saw her twin flush.

'I suppose you mean Malcolm Sutton,' she said, her tone defensive. 'As it happens, I care a lot about him. He's very big in property development, and he's worth a fortune.'

'Are you in love with him?'

Trina shrugged. 'I don't know, but it's fun finding out.' She regarded Danni seriously. 'Why are men such a problem? For them, life is a *smorgasbord*, but we women are supposed to settle for one dish.'

Danni didn't know how to answer this, so she said nothing.

Still Trina pressed her point. 'Rowan and I will never see eye-to-eye on this. I guess it's because of his mother.'

In spite of herself, Danni was curious. 'What does his mother have to do with it?'

'She ran off with some man when Rowan was a teenager. I guess that's why he's afraid to let any woman off the leash.'

Danni lapsed into thoughtful silence. No wonder Rowan was so angry over Trina's behaviour and their attempt to deceive him! Knowing his past, how could Trina treat his feelings so callously? Anger seeped into Danni's voice. 'However you feel about Rowan, he still expects you to finish the assignment. There's obviously nothing wrong with your health.'

Trina coloured with embarrassment, but her expression became stubborn. 'My chest pains were real enough. As you well know, with my medical history...'

Danni held up her hands. 'Stop it. You aren't holding that damned rescue over my head again! All right, you saved my life and I'm eternally grateful, but it isn't going to change matters this time.'

Trina had the grace to look chastened. 'I accept that. But I still can't complete the assignment. Malcolm and I are leaving for the Gold Coast tomorrow.'

'Can't you postpone the trip?'

'I can't, Danni, or I would. Malcolm's parents have flown in from America just to meet me, and I can't let them down.'

Not when it was easier to let her sister down, Danni thought crossly. But she knew she was going to let Trina get away with it, all the same. To her chagrin, she found she had been hoping that Trina would say no. Against all common sense, Danni was glad that she and Rowan would be working together again.

A knock on the door startled them both, then Rowan's voice penetrated the timber. 'Danni, are you all right?'

Trina gripped Danni's arm. 'Don't tell him I was here, please?'

Her expression grim, Danni nodded. If Rowan still cared for Trina, he would be hurt if he met her on the arm of another man. Danni could spare him that, at least. Pushing Trina out of sight behind the door, she opened it a crack. 'I'm all right, I just came in here to fix my dress.' Before he could inspect the office, she stepped out and closed the door behind her. Then she took Rowan's arm. 'There's a photo I want to discuss with you. It's in the other room.'

Rowan allowed her to lead him through the thinning crowd until they came to a large, framed portrait. 'This one,' she said without looking at it.

'Are you sure it's this one?' He turned her around and, to her horror, she realised she was staring at the portrait of the old woman feeding the pigeons.

'I . . . er . . . it's the one over there.' She pointed at random.

'That's a sign saying "Fire Escape",' he informed her solemnly, adding, 'Do you think Trina has had enough time to escape by now?'

She collapsed against the wall, feeling defeated. 'You saw her?'

'And the American businessman she came with.'

'Oh.' The small sound escaped her pursed lips.

To her surprise, she noticed that Rowan was smiling. 'It's all right,' he reassured her. 'I told you it was over between us, so it doesn't matter to me if she's seeing someone else.'

'I didn't want you to be hurt,' she admitted, feeling foolish.

He touched her chin with a crooked finger, tilting her head until their eyes met. 'I know, and I appreciate your concern for my feelings. But you were worrying needlessly.'

'But what about the photos?' she asked anxiously.

His gentle expression shifted to one of concern. 'I suppose I'll have to hire another model, and re-shoot the catalogue from scratch.'

'Am I really so hopeless?' she asked in a small voice.

He stared at her, stunned surprise etched on his face. 'Of course you're not hopeless. But your time is too valuable to waste modelling swimsuits.'

'Your time isn't too precious to photograph them,' she reminded him shyly.

'Then you don't mind finishing the job?'

Relief and pleasure made her cheeks glow with warmth. 'I don't mind. I thought you preferred Trina to me.'

'She's a more experienced model,' he explained. 'But that's her only advantage over you.'

He couldn't know how happy his words made her, and she drifted through the remainder of the evening on a cloud of contentment. Rowan had been afraid she was too good for the assignment, not the other way around. They would be working together again, after all.

Next morning, she awoke feeling less optimistic. Trina had lost interest in Rowan but Danni still wasn't convinced by Rowan's assurance. Until she *was* sure, there was the nagging fear that he saw her as a substitute for her twin.

On the way to Rowan's studio, she passed a news stand. On it was displayed the magazine featuring Trina's photographs. The centrefold was not displayed, of course, but the pictures on the cover were provocative enough to make Danni look away in discomfort. Seeing Trina's pictures was like looking into a mirror and seeing a distorted reflection of herself. The pictures looked like her, and yet she could never have posed like that in a million years.

She wondered if the centrefold had caused the rift between Rowan and Trina. It was hard to imagine any man being pleased about such a thing.

The question stayed with her as they worked together, but there was no chance to talk until the lunch break, when Rowan sent out for food for them. Watching him excise a crescent of sandwich with his perfect white teeth, she felt an ache start up deep inside her. It was as if each bite was connecting with the tender skin of her neck. She could feel each nip, feel his firm mouth as it roved over her throat in a torrent of love bites. Suddenly, his head came up and his eyes locked with hers, making her colour hotly, as if she had somehow communicated her fantasy to him. But all he said was, 'I'm glad you came back today, Danielle.'

'My friends call me Danni,' she said in a husky voice.

'Very well—Danni.'

So he wanted to be her friend. The idea warmed her anew, until she reminded herself that friendship was very different from the relationship he had had with Trina.

Suddenly, she realised how much she was taking for granted. Why was she assuming that he and Trina had been lovers? For she realised that was what she was presuming. The idea was acutely disturbing, but safer than assuming too little and then finding out the truth later on.

'What did you think of Trina doing the centrefold?' she asked abruptly, trying to keep the anxiety out of her voice.

He shrugged non-committally. 'It's her body. Surely she can do with it what she likes? If we had been more involved, I might have felt differently.'

He didn't know it, but he was giving her the answer she had hardly dared to anticipate. 'But surely it's hypocritical to do your kind of work all day, then object when the model is...is someone close to you,' she persisted recklessly.

He thought for a moment. 'I prefer to think that someone I respected would respect my feelings enough, so the issue wouldn't arise,' he said finally.

But the question *had* arisen. Despite the fact that he was going out with Trina, she had gone ahead and posed for the centrefold. It was obvious that he disapproved of it, but whether it was because he cared for Trina, she couldn't decide. 'Did you know she was doing the spread?' she asked curiously.

He crushed his sandwich wrappers with an aggressive gesture, tossed them into a wastebasket and returned to his camera. 'What does it matter now? She did it, didn't she? Now, are we going to discuss Trina all day, or are you going to model the blue sarong for me?'

Still baffled, Danni went behind the makeshift screen and slipped on the satiny one-piece garment. It was strapless, but the bra top was underwired so that it moulded her well-formed breasts and accentuated her slim waist.

There was no more talk of any kind as, for the next hour, Rowan directed her movements while his camera whirred. The flashlights popped repeatedly, until she was dazzled. Eventually he snapped off the spotlights under their silver, umbrella-like reflectors, and she relaxed, massaging her eyes.

'Are you all right?' he asked as he noticed her action.

She let her hand drop to her side. 'I'm all right.'

But he would have none of her assurances. Moving to her side, he tilted her head back and lifted first one eyelid and then the other with gently probing fingers. Tears sprang to her eyes as they met the light again. 'Why didn't you tell me the lights were affecting your eyes?' he demanded.

'I didn't want to be a nuisance. I'm sure Trina wouldn't have complained about such a thing.'

'Bother Trina!' he exploded. 'She's used to these conditions.' He regarded her intently. 'Why are you trying so hard to be her, when there's no longer any need?'

Because she didn't know which of them he would prefer to be working with, she acknowledged to herself. Since he was waiting for an answer, she said aloud, 'I'm just trying to do a good job.'

'And you're succeeding,' he assured her. 'You don't have to be a Trina clone. You have your own way of selling a shot, and I rather like it.'

Anxious not to let him see how absurdly important his praise was to her, she dropped her long lashes over her smarting eyes. He placed an arm around her shoulders and steered her to a canvas chair. 'Sit here with your eyes closed, I won't be a minute,' he told her.

Still basking in the glow of his approval, she relaxed in the chair, only then realising how tired she was. The strain of trying to master all the tricks of the modelling trade in a few days was telling on her. Or was it the strain of working with Rowan, knowing how strongly she was attracted to him, yet not being sure enough of him to do anything about it?

She started as the subject of her thoughts came back. 'What are you doing?' she asked as he tilted her head back and held it there.

'I can't have you developing eye strain,' he said. Then he parted her eyelids gently, and she felt cool drops filming her burning eyes. 'This will take some of the soreness away,' he explained.

'Thank you. It already feels better.'

'It was the least I could do, since I was the cause of your discomfort.'

In more ways than one! she thought ruefully. While she waited for the drops to take effect, she

let her thoughts wander. Dimly, she could hear
Rowan pottering around the studio.

Cradled in the comfortable chair with her eyes
closed, she began to doze until Rowan shook her
awake. 'Isn't it time you got changed?' he asked,
his voice oddly hoarse.

She had forgotten that she was still wearing the
skimpy sarong, and she felt waves of heat suffuse
her as she saw Rowan surveying the large amount
of tanned thigh her pose revealed. Hastily, she stood
up.

'How do your eyes feel?' he asked, amusement
playing across his strong features.

'They're fine now that the drops have worked,'
she said, discomfited by his obvious interest in her.
He might well be looking at her and seeing Trina,
but her responses were very much her own.

'I'd better get dressed,' she stammered.

But his eyes darkened as he took a step towards
her. 'I suppose you should.' But his voice carried
no real conviction. 'On the other hand...'

'There's no other hand,' she said determinedly.
Held spellbound by his gaze, it was becoming ever
more difficult to remember her resolution not to
get involved with any man of Trina's, past or
present. How could she ever be sure which of them
he was seeing when he looked at her?

A moan of anguish escaped her lips as his finger
traced a line down the side of her face. 'Are you
sure there's no other hand?' he asked.

'No, there can't be,' she tried again. 'You and
Trina...'

'...dated for a while and that was it,' he said firmly. 'You seem to be having some trouble accepting the fact.'

'Then you and she weren't...you never...' Damn it, why couldn't she come out and say it?

He did it for her. 'We weren't lovers, if that's what's bothering you. I didn't feel inclined to get in a queue.'

Even while she felt relief wash over her, Danni was still troubled. She was too afraid of the answer to ask him how he felt about Trina now. 'How do you know I'm not the same?' she asked, her throat so tight, it was an effort to force the words out.

'Because you're quite different from her,' he said seriously. 'You have more compassion in your little finger than she has in her whole body. I've already seen enough of you to know that you care about people. You could never collect scalps on a belt the way she does.'

'But you *did* mistake me for her,' she reminded him.

'Only that first time at Monarch Magazines, when I was exhausted after an all-day shoot. Never for an instant since then.' Cupping her chin, he tilted her face up to his and fixed her with a penetrating inspection. 'You're your own woman, Danielle O'Dare, not a carbon copy of someone else. Is that how you're afraid I see you?'

'It's how people have seen Trina and me all our lives,' she confessed shakily, stunned by the depth of his awareness.

'God, what must that be like?' he breathed. 'Having a double walking beside you through life, so you're never quite sure of yourself as an individual.'

With an attempt at lightness, she said, 'It has its good side, too. I never feel totally alone. There's always one other person who shares my thoughts and feelings.'

'And your lovers?' he asked, his eyes still fixed on her face.

She drew a strangled breath. 'Sometimes.'

'So that's what you're so afraid of. You think I'm interested in you as a substitute for your twin, sort of keeping me warm until she's back on the scene.'

'It wouldn't be the first time,' she said, injecting a hollow laugh into her voice.

In the afternoon light, the planes and angles of Rowan's face were accentuated, giving him an even more hawkish look. 'I would never make that mistake.' He took a slowly indrawn breath. 'And to convince you, I'd like to kiss you—on the understanding that I know exactly who is in my arms.'

What more assurance did she need? She nodded and held her breath as he bent towards her.

His mouth was hard and firm, and she gasped as his tongue teased at her lips, urging them apart so he could kiss her deeply. But before she could give herself fully to his embrace he drew away, then kissed her again, his mouth darting away and back again until she felt as if she would explode with the force of the sensations he was arousing.

With a gasp of frustration, she clamped her arms around his shoulders and held him against her so she could taste the heady fullness of his kiss. After those tantalising, butterfly kisses, the final onslaught was overwhelming.

Passion radiated around them like a living thing. It must have been building up inside him as powerfully as it had been in her, she realised in astonished delight.

As her hands slid under the knitted fabric of his T-shirt and roved over his hair-strewn chest, his breathing quickened. Moulded against him, she was breathlessly aware of his growing desire for her. While she had been bedevilled by fantasies about him, he must have felt the same way. 'I've been wanting to do this all day,' he said, as if in answer to her thought.

She didn't even feel shy in confessing, 'Me, too.'

He murmured a pleased response against her hairline, sending shivers of pleasure down her spine. 'Only being able to look at you through my camera lens, wearing those skimpy swimsuits, was like a kind of torture. I can hardly believe you're in my arms. You know, I feel as if I've known you for much longer than these few days we've been working together.'

Although she nestled against him in silent agreement, she felt a sudden chill of fear which was not dispelled by the warmth of his embrace. In a sense, he *had* known her for a long time—or, at least, her mirror image. How could she be sure that wasn't what gave him this sense of familiarity? Far from reassuring her, his words brought alive her worst fears. In breaking her long-standing resolution not to get involved with any man who had dated Trina, was she making the greatest mistake of her life?

CHAPTER SIX

DANNI awoke to the jangling of her alarm clock, and blearily reached to shut it off. Then she looked askance at the time. The alarm should have gone off an hour ago. She must have forgotten to wind it fully when she'd set it last night.

In a panic, she leapt out of bed. Rowan would be arriving to collect her for the day's work soon. She barely had time to shower and dress.

His Mercedes was parked outside her block of flats when she skipped downstairs less than half an hour later. 'You're out of breath. Been rushing?' he observed when she climbed in beside him.

'My alarm let me down,' she explained. 'I hope this outfit will do?' Luckily, she had set her clothes out the night before, so getting dressed hadn't been a problem.

He cast his eye over her cotton mesh top and basque-tucked cotton skirt, sashed with a hessian belt, and nodded his approval. 'You look great. The kangaroos are going to be bounding with delight.'

His bad joke made her wince. 'I thought it was bad form to perform with children or animals.'

'That advice was for actors,' he told her. 'All you have to do today is pose among the native animals to add colour to the catalogue.'

He made it sound so easy, Danni reflected. She would be surprised if it turned out to be so. Already, her short career as a model had taught her that looking casually glamorous was hard work indeed. But she was still looking forward to the day of shooting at Taronga Zoo. It would be a welcome change from swimwear.

The zoo staff were expecting them, and they were allowed to drive into the grounds with their cumbersome photographic equipment. 'Is Tony joining us here?' she asked Rowan as she helped him to unload everything.

'He's back at the darkroom, processing the last batch of film,' he informed her. 'Today, it's just you and me.'

Just you and me. The idea was curiously thrilling, and she felt a shiver of anticipation. She could hardly believe they were here together, in such a glorious setting. Work had always satisfied her, but working with someone as creative and demanding as Rowan had added a new dimension to the experience for her.

She swung around, soaking up Taronga's special atmosphere. The zoo was magnificently situated on a wooded hillside, and the sparkling vastness of Sydney Harbour lay in a jewelled carpet at their feet. She hadn't been to the zoo for years, and now she was delighted to find that the old-fashioned cages had been replaced by modern, naturalistic enclosures.

The kangaroo enclosure was their first stop, and there were no bars in front of the meadow-like area to spoil Rowan's shot of Danni feeding the docile animals. An Old Man Kangaroo appraised her from beneath hooded eyelids, which gave it a sleepy appearance, then got to its feet and lumbered up to inspect her outstretched hand. She had been provided with special cereal with which to feed the animals, but they were too well-fed to show any interest in her offerings. Luckily, Rowan snapped off a shot of the 'roo inspecting her hand, and pronounced himself satisfied.

The chimpanzee park, with its rolling hills and trees for the animals to climb, provided a backdrop for another shot. 'Not for the catalogue, for my next showing,' Rowan explained when she reminded him that chimpanzees could hardly be classed as 'native fauna'.

The thought of her pictures being featured in an exhibition pleased her, for she knew now that Rowan would do an outstanding job of it. Furtively, she switched her gaze from the animals to him. Head bent over his camera, he looked virile and handsome, his capable hands working the expensive equipment with a sureness which awed her. Then he looked up and she was caught in his compelling gaze, as if someone had directed a spotlight on to her. She blinked, momentarily dazzled, then realised he was speaking to her. 'I'm sorry?'

'You were miles away,' he laughed and she coloured. 'I said we should head for the koala enclosure while the sun's in the right position.'

The koala house had been designed 'in the round', so that visitors were on a level with the treetops and could see the koalas in their natural surroundings. A newly arrived koala, tamer than those already on show, was provided for Danni to hold in a photograph. 'Just watch the sharp claws,'

the keeper cautioned as he handed her the furry
animal.

She did as bidden, posing this way and that with
the sleepy creature until Rowan pronounced himself
satisfied. As she handed the koala back to its
keeper, she noticed that moving had suddenly
become an effort, and the air had developed a
swimming quality. 'What's next?' she asked Rowan,
hearing her voice coming from far away.

He looked at her in concern. 'Are you feeling all
right?'

She passed a hand across her eyes. 'It's standing
out in the hot sun that's made me feel so light-
headed. I feel...'

She swayed and he wrapped an arm around her,
leading her to a bench so she could sit down. 'Why
didn't you say you weren't feeling well?'

'I was fine until a few minutes ago,' she insisted.
'I'll feel better when I've eaten something.'

He made a disapproving noise in his throat.
'Don't tell me you left home without having
breakfast?'

She gestured weakly. 'The alarm was late going
off, and I didn't want to keep you waiting.'

'Of all the foolish...' he exploded, then calmed
himself. 'Do you think I'm such an ogre that I
couldn't have waited while you had breakfast?'

The dizziness had passed and she looked up at
him, her gaze softening. 'I don't think you're an
ogre at all,' she said softly, hardly aware of having
spoken aloud until she saw the tremor of response
which shook him.

'Don't look at me like that,' he said gruffly.

'Like what?'

'Like a puppy who doesn't know if I'm going to kick it or fondle it. You should know me better than that by now.'

She was starting to, enough to know that he might seem aggressive and tough, but it was mainly where his work was concerned. Underneath, he was tender and considerate.

He proved it yet again by insisting on taking her to lunch in the zoo's restaurant before they did any more work. After the meal of grilled steak and salad, she felt refreshed and ready to go on.

'No, I've got all the background shots I need now,' he demurred. 'And I don't want you collapsing on me from overwork.'

She let her breath out in a sigh of relief. 'I'm fine now, but I had no idea that looking glamorous all the time was such hard work.'

He paused in the act of covering his camera lens. 'You don't need to work at it. Maybe at mastering the technique, but not at looking good. The camera loves you.'

But what about Rowan Traynor? she wondered. How did he feel about her, away from the lights and whirr of his camera? She was aware of a new closeness between them since they had started working together, but would it last now that the assignment was ending?

His next words dispelled some of her doubts. 'Since I'm the one who starved you and exposed you to sunstroke, how about if I make amends by offering you a swim at my place?'

'Won't I be putting your housekeeper out, arriving unannounced?' she asked.

'It's Dora's afternoon off today. In any case, I've told her who you are, if that's what's worrying you.'

It was, and she smiled her relief. 'In that case, a swim sounds lovely right now,' she agreed.

When they reached Rowan's penthouse, Dora Howard was just leaving for the afternoon, but she greeted Danni enthusiastically. 'It's lovely to see you again, dear. Such a likeness to young Trina, though. I can't get over it. I was so sure you were her when you came here the other day with that terrible Andrews man.'

A pang shot through Danni. It sounded as if Trina had been a frequent visitor to Rowan's apartment. 'It's all right, we're used to people mixing us up,' she told Mrs Howard.

'I'm sure. Well, it was nice meeting you ... er ... Danni.' She went off, still shaking her head.

When she realised that they were finally alone in Rowan's penthouse, Danni's breath caught in her throat and her heart began to gather speed. They had been alone often during the assignment, but work had always come first. Now the work was behind them. How would she fit in to Rowan's life now—if she fitted in at all?

There was also the question of his feelings towards Trina. He still referred to experiences he'd shared with Trina, as if expecting Danni to know about them. What was she to make of him?

But this afternoon belonged only to her, and she was crazy to let her anxiety get in the way. She fixed a smile on her face and turned to him. 'You mentioned that we could swim, but I didn't see any pool the last time I was here.'

He laughed. 'I doubt whether you were in any frame of mind to appreciate the finer features of my home.'

She joined in the laughter, glad that they could see the whole thing as a joke now. 'You're right, I wasn't.'

With a courtly gesture, he allowed her to precede him up the last flight of stairs to the topmost level of the penthouse. She hadn't come this far last time, and now she saw that the level opened on to a wide, sun-drenched terrace, with a compact freeform pool in the centre.

'I expected a communal pool shared by all the owners in the building,' she said, surprise in her voice.

'This terrace and the pool were the main attractions of the place for me. I don't care much for communal living.'

That didn't surprise her. She had already gained an impression of him as a lone wolf, a man who could walk among crowds and still be alone, yet not lonely. He was... she searched for the right word... self-contained.

He gave her a playful push towards the terrace, and she stepped through a pair of sliding glass doors on to a pebble-surfaced area. North Sydney lay spread out at their feet. She could see all the way to the misty Blue Mountains. So close she felt as if she could touch it, was the jewel-like expanse of Sydney Harbour, its surface dotted with pleasure-boats. The Sydney Opera House looked like the grandest of them, its white sails appearing to billow in the gentle breeze.

She turned shining eyes to him. 'It's breath-taking!'

But his eyes were on her alone as he said, 'Definitely.' He turned away abruptly. 'I'll fix us some drinks.'

She already felt intoxicated by the magic of the setting and Rowan's nearness, but she accepted the gin and tonic he made for her, needing something to occupy her restless hands.

Seated opposite Rowan, under a gaily striped umbrella, Danni was grateful for the cool glass which kept her fingers occupied. Otherwise she knew they would slide across the table to link with Rowan's. The need to touch him was almost over-powering, and she closed her eyes against the strength of it.

'Is the sun in your eyes? I can tilt the umbrella.'

'No, I'm fine, really.' If she didn't count the family of butterflies which were nesting in her stomach, she reflected. What had happened to the cool, hard-headed reporter? She felt like a hot-headed teenager. What had Rowan done to her?

'Penny for them,' he said, startling her.

'I was thinking about you,' she blurted out, then felt her face flame. She hadn't meant to admit any such thing.

'And that's a problem?' he queried.

'It is for me. Oh, Rowan, I don't need any com-plications right now.'

'Is that what I am, a complication?'

'Yes—oh, yes,' she acknowledged. He was getting in the way of her single-minded approach to journalism. And she still doubted whether it was her or Trina he saw when he looked at her.

'Good. At least it means you feel something for me.'

'How can I? I don't even know you.'

'Sometimes biographical details don't mean as much as instinctive reactions,' he said. 'But I can remedy the first problem. What would you like to know?'

Thankful to have the conversation on safe ground, she asked, 'Did you always want to be a photographer?'

'I always wanted to earn my living with a camera, but fashion is just a means to that end. I enjoy it and it's provided most of this.' He gestured around the terrace. 'But it's transitory. I want my work to contribute to a record of our times. Does that sound grandiose?'

'Not at all. I think every writer feels the same, whether they admit it or not.'

He looked pleased. 'I'm glad you understand. The only other person who did was my father.'

'Is he a photographer, too?'

'Was,' he corrected. 'He died a couple of years ago.' He forestalled her attempt at sympathy. 'It's all right. He went the way he would have wished to, on assignment in South America. He was working in San Salvador and was caught in an earthquake.'

Was that why Rowan's own photographs of war zones reflected a dislike of conflict? War had taken his father to South America, even though it was a natural disaster which claimed his life. 'Was he away a lot when you were young?' she asked.

'Some,' he agreed. 'But he also had a studio in North Sydney, near where mine is now. While I was growing up, he stayed at home and did portrait photography. His heart wasn't in it, but he did it for me. I just hope I was worth it.'

'He must have thought so.' And I do, too, she added. While they talked, her hand had relaxed, and now lay a hair's breadth away from his, so she could feel the warmth emanating from him. Slowly, her fingers crept towards his, and he curled her hand into his palm. Her heartbeat gathered speed, and it was an effort to continue the conversation. 'It seems we both had fathers whose hearts were elsewhere,' she admitted. 'Mine dreamed of being an Irish bard. Luckily, he was able to follow his dream.'

'Is he in Ireland now?'

She nodded. 'A distant relative left my parents a small farm in Cork. They didn't think they could afford to go, but then Dad was offered a teaching post at University College, so they went together. Now their letters are full of their adventures and Dad's poetry.'

'Well, at least they were able to follow their dream together,' Rowan said, disturbing her with the bitterness which edged his voice. 'That was a luxury my father never knew.'

She debated whether to tell him what Trina had already told her, then decided to let him explain in his own way and time.

Remembering the harmony between her parents, it seemed she was more fortunate than Rowan. Her mother had defended her father's right to dream, no matter what it had cost her. She had confessed to Danni that she hated leaving her daughters, grown up or not, but she would never have let Sean go without her.

'I suppose I should be thankful that Dad was around when I was growing up,' Rowan said gruffly. 'And, despite her flaws, my mother was beautiful too. She had the kind of personality which draws men like magnets.' His voice became distant. 'I wasn't supposed to know about her affairs, but I worked it out. At first, Dad stayed around, hoping it would help, but it didn't, so he gave up the studio and went back to the front-lines.'

Hearing the pain in his voice, Danni ached for a way to ease the memories for him. She understood now why he couldn't condone Trina's behaviour, knowing only too well the heartache it brought.

He surprised her by laughing harshly. 'Still, I can understand what Dad saw in my mother. She was always full of life and refused to take anything seriously.'

Like Trina, Danni thought. She had the same fun-loving temperament as Rowan's mother. But she also had the same flaws which had destroyed his parents' marriage. 'Some people can't help behaving like that,' she said quietly. 'They don't mean to hurt anyone.'

He seemed to know that she was talking more about Trina than his mother. 'I know,' he agreed.

'That's why I count myself lucky to have found you in time.'

In time for what? To stop him making the same mistake as his father? She felt a glow of satisfaction at the idea.

Their hands were still linked, and he stroked her forearm slowly, sending shivers of sensation through her. She leaned towards him as if pulled on an invisible string, feeling fiercely hungry. But it was a hunger which no food could satisfy. Rowan's dark eyes slid over her, his expression telling her he felt the same way.

As one, they leaned closer, until their lips met across the table. Rowan's hands gripped her shoulders and she linked her arms around his neck. The edge of the table bit into her, and she pulled back reluctantly, grudging every inch which kept them apart.

Desire swept through her so strongly that, when she stood up, she had to hold on to the table for support. She nodded, not yet trusting her voice, which would surely betray her with its huskiness. She could feel her throat tight and her mouth dry, so that it was an effort to speak. 'I think we'd better have that swim, don't you?'

Her fingers were shaking so much that she had trouble changing into the bikini which Rowan had brought for her from the studio. It was crocheted from crimson cotton over a flesh-coloured lining, giving the impression that it was almost transparent. Catching sight of herself in it in the changing-room mirror, she felt bold and wanton, understanding why the design was called 'Temptress'. It was exactly what she felt like.

When she emerged, Rowan was waiting for her. For a moment, he stood still, his eyes drinking in the sight of her. Under his intense scrutiny, she felt proud that the bikini was so skimpy. In it, she felt the power of her sex, a novel and amazingly enjoyable sensation. She drew herself up to her full height, so that her breasts were thrust forward. She heard Rowan's indrawn breath of admiration.

Then it was her turn. As if drawn on invisible wires, her eyes travelled along the line of his breastbone, across the dark chest hair which tapered to a V, making him seem even more lean and athletic than usual. His broad, muscular chest narrowed to a slim waist and long, powerful legs.

As she watched, he dived cleanly into the pool, judging the depth with practised accuracy so that he surfaced just short of the far wall. Resting his arm along the coping, he swept his glistening hair back from his eyes and watched her approach.

Under his gaze, she felt suddenly shy, which was at odds with the wantonness she'd felt only a moment before. She balked at jumping into the water with him, aware that, once she did, there would be no turning back.

'Are you coming in?' he asked.

'Yes,' she said firmly, recognising that the decision had been made as soon as she agreed to come here with him today. Her work, Trina, all might have ceased to exist. All she could think about was how much she longed for Rowan to take her in his arms.

She swam across the pool to him, having trouble co-ordinating her breathing enough to swim with her usual grace. When she reached him, his eyes were alight with desire for her. Instead of going into his arms, she hooked her own arms over the hand-rail behind her and stretched her legs out in front until her toes peeped out of the water.

She let out a yelp as Rowan made a dive for them, taking her big toe in his mouth. Like a big dog, he worried it until she almost slid under the water. Before she could sink, he caught her in strong arms and clasped her to his streaming chest. 'It's all right, I saved you.'

Linking her arms around his neck, she smiled back. 'Yes, but saved me for what?'

'This.' His mouth closed over hers, coaxing a response she hadn't known was waiting for him until now. Distantly, she heard a sighing sound, which she realised came from her own throat. Being in Rowan's arms like this felt so right that it was as if she had come home after a long journey.

His quickened breathing told her he felt the same way. Together, they drifted on to the wide curving step at the shallow end of the pool and Rowan slid his hands along her slick body until she felt every nerve-ending vibrate in response. Almost of their own accord, her hands skidded across his wet back and came to rest there, drawing him closer to her as the water lapped hypnotically around them.

She pressed hungry lips against his throat, feeling the throb of his pulsebeat under her mouth. In turn, he sought the pink curve of her ear and kissed the droplets of water beading it, then threaded his tongue into the shell-like opening, until response surged through her like a rising tide.

When he had first kissed her at his studio, so long ago, he had set her senses on fire. She had believed they had crested the peak of sensation then, but it was as nothing compared with the heights he was taking her to now.

At what moment they discarded their swimsuits, she was only dimly aware, but suddenly their clothes were floating nearby, and there were no more impediments to the impossibly sweet sensation of skin touching skin as their bodies moulded together. Then there was simply no more time for conscious reasoning.

She had never dreamed that making love underwater could be so beautiful or breathtakingly sensuous as it proved to be. The water made their bodies light and their movements utterly fluid. When he moved inside her, she felt as if she was drifting on a cloud of sensation.

She was a mermaid and he was her merman. They were gloriously weightless, moving as they chose. One minute, Rowan hovered over her, the next, they lay entwined, side by side in the shallows. Around them, a tidal wave of joy grew and grew, until finally it crashed over them, carrying them before it in a mindless rush of sensation.

When at last she could focus again, Danni rested against the curving step, letting the water settle around her as their movements no longer disturbed the rippling surface. Rowan kept one arm around her and the other braced against the coping. Their legs floated out in front of them. Comparing his muscular brown ones with her own lightly tanned pair, she thought she might look the same, but everything else about her felt as if it was changed.

'Wonderful,' breathed Rowan at last.

'Mmm-hmm,' she agreed, the writer in her for once lost for words.

He kissed her lightly. 'I never want to make love on dry land again.'

She laughed, feeling more alive than at any time before. 'I know. But if I stay too long, I'll have skin like orange peel.'

He took her hand, turning it palm upwards so he could inspect the damage. 'It doesn't matter to me, you're still beautiful. But you're right, we should get out now.'

He helped her out of the water and wrapped a bath sheet around her, massaging her limbs with slow, sensuous movements. As his hands worked down her body, she felt her desire building again and her breathing quickened.

He had also lit the fuse of his own desire, she saw, as he dropped the towel and pulled her against him. Then he swept her into his arms, ignoring her cry of protest.

'I can walk.'

'I like you this way,' he insisted. 'I can have you just where I want you.'

As she realised that he was taking her into his bedroom, she buried her face in his neck. God, what had happened to her today? She felt like a creature of clay, which Rowan was free to mould to his heart's desire.

By the time he set her down on his vast bed, they were both barely able to breathe. When he leaned over her, she opened herself to him willingly, wanting more and more of his possession, until her world was filled with him. Then there would be no room for doubts or fears.

But he wasn't about to let her off lightly. With maddening slowness, he knelt on the bed above her, allowing his hands to trail across her breasts and stomach, until she felt weak with the need of him.

'Danni?' he said, in a tone that was more a statement than a question.

'Yes, yes,' she repeated over and over. Couldn't he see how this was driving all reason from her?

It was evidently the response he wanted. 'Yes,' he said softly, and leaned over her.

But before he could complete the movement, the spell was shattered as the telephone shrilled throughout the room.

'Damn!' he muttered, half turning towards the sound.

'Let it ring, Rowan, please,' she begged. He had inflamed her to such heights that she couldn't stand the thought of being left alone, even for a few seconds.

But he rolled off the bed and tied a towel around his hips. 'I'll make it quick,' he promised.

She had never felt so bereft. It was as if a part of her had been torn away. She ached for him, feeling her eyes brim with tears as she heard him move into the dressing-room and pick up the phone.

As she lay, quivering with expectancy, she heard his voice sharpen, and unwillingly focused on the sound. What was making him so angry? 'For crying out loud, Tony, isn't there anything you can do?'

Alarm started her heart racing. Something must be wrong at the studio for Rowan to sound so furious. She was sitting up waiting for him when he returned. 'What is it?'

He sat down heavily on the edge of the bed. 'There's something chemically wrong with the film we used to shoot the catalogue covers. They won't process. They'll have to be reshot.' He slammed one fist against the other in agitation. 'Damn it, I should have supervised the job myself!'

Instead of coming here with her, she finished mentally, feeling a pang of guilt. Then common sense returned. He hadn't done anything he hadn't wanted to do.

'What are you going to do?' she asked.

His dark eyes met hers. Worry made them seem even more hooded and mysterious than usual. 'What can I do? I'll have to set the whole thing up and do the shots again. We've lost two whole days, and the deadline is looming, so there's no alternative.'

Her loving companion of the last few hours had been replaced by a stranger. From eager, teasing lover, he had turned into tough professional as he ticked off on his fingers everything he would need to do to complete the reshoot in the time that was left.

A chill went through her as she watched him change before her eyes. She tried to tell herself she was imagining things. He was only reacting to an emergency like the well-schooled professional he was. She would do the same if it was a journalistic crisis.

Although her body ached with unfulfilled desire, she made her voice deliberately brisk, so as not to distract him from his task. 'Is there anything I can do?'

He hardly seemed to hear the question, but nodded, his eyes fixed on a distant point. Then he marshalled his thoughts with an obvious effort and turned to her. 'There's nothing you can do right now, Trina. Before I can use you again, I'll have to round up the costumes and props and give Tony a hand to set it all up again. We should be ready for you first thing in the morning.'

CHAPTER SEVEN

DANNI sat frozen on the bed for at least a minute before she recovered sufficiently from the shock of his words to respond.

'I'm not Trina.'

Distracted, he raked a hand through his hair. 'For God's sake, woman, what difference does it make? Can you be here for the new shots tomorrow or not?'

Dumbly, she nodded, too devastated to trust her voice. Without another word, he returned to his dressing-room and she heard him rummaging around. When he came out, he was fully clothed. 'I've got to get back to the studio and see if there's any hope of salvaging the film. Ring for a taxi to take you home and put it on my account, all right? I'm sorry about ruining your evening, but you know how it is.'

Then he was gone. At last she was alone to think about what had just happened. She understood how worried he was about the ruined film and the pressing deadline, worried enough to call her Trina by mistake. What she couldn't, *wouldn't* understand, was his dismissal of it as unimportant. 'What difference does it make?' he had said. Surely he knew that it made a great deal of difference to her? She had explained her fear of men using her as a stand-in for Trina. After Keith Bowden, she had vowed never to put herself in that situation again.

Foolishly letting her heart rule her head, she had broken her vow, and look where it had got her! Under pressure, Rowan forgot which twin he was dealing with, and when she pointed out his mistake he dismissed it as trivial.

Except that it wasn't, to her. Maybe he had so many women in his life that he had trouble keeping track of them. It was at odds with his assertion that he was a one-woman man. Maybe he meant one at a time, she thought bitterly.

But not this time.

She dressed quickly, then located her handbag and rang for a taxi, but she balked at charging it to Rowan's account. Right now, she didn't want to owe him anything.

By the time she got home, her mood had swung from misery to anger. How dared he treat her like this? His career was important to him—more important than she was, it seemed. Well, two could play that game. Maybe it was time she got on with her own career, and her life.

When she got home, her answering machine was on and she debated whether to play the calls back or leave them until morning. Remembering her resolution, she switched the machine on. The message was from Ray Conreid, her old editor at the investment magazine. He wanted her to call him back today, even if it was late when she returned.

She glanced at the clock. It was late by her standards, but not by Ray's. He was a night owl, turning up at the office at all hours when he couldn't sleep. Curiously, she dialled his number.

'It's Danni, I hope I didn't wake you,' she said when he answered.

'Not at all. I'm glad you called back.' There was a slight pause. 'I don't know if I have any right to ask for your help after the way we treated you, but I'm in urgent need of a writer for an out-of-town assignment.'

His call was like the answer to a prayer. 'Of course I'm interested,' she said at once. 'Besides, it wasn't your fault that I left. It was my own decision.'

He let out an audible sigh of relief. 'I'm so glad you feel that way. Now that our casual journalist has moved into your old spot, I don't have anyone to send out on special assignments, and I'm really stuck. I take it you haven't found anything permanent yet?'

'I have some feelers out, but there's no hurry. Actually, I've been doing a spot of modelling,' she said casually.

He chuckled softly. 'Next thing, you'll be telling me it really *was* you in that centrefold.'

Ray's gentle teasing came like a breath of fresh air after the intensity of the last few days with Rowan. 'You'll just have to wonder. Now, what's the urgent assignment?'

Instantly, he was all business. 'Mrs Philmont wants us to do a feature on the small wineries of the Hunter Valley, the Pitt Street lawyers, the weekend farmers, that kind of thing. One of her friends is a winemaker there and gave her the idea.'

More than anything, she felt a need to put some distance between herself and Rowan. Thinking of him brought another thought to her mind. 'Who'll be taking the pictures?'

'Donna Healey. You've worked with her before.'

'I remember. We worked well together.'

'I thought so. Look, I'd like you to get started on this as soon as possible. When can we get together for a briefing?'

She thought furiously. Rowan was expecting her at his studio tomorrow to reshoot the catalogue covers. Although she was sorely tempted, her conscience wouldn't allow her to let him down, no matter how she felt about him on a personal level. 'Would the day after tomorrow do?' she asked Ray.

'It will have to. Meanwhile, I'll get things moving, so you can head for the Hunter straight after our meeting. I hate to rush you like this, but you know what Mrs P is like when she gets an idea in her head.'

'You're asking me that?' she said with a laugh as she hung up the phone. Well, at least Mrs Philmont was doing Danni a good turn this time. Rowan was still very much on her mind, and she had just had ample proof of how dangerous that was. An out-of-town writing assignment was just what she needed to get away and think things over.

She debated whether to share her plans with Rowan when she arrived at the studio next morning, then thought better of it. He was in a vile mood, whether because of the ruined film, or over his behaviour last night, she wasn't sure. She doubted whether it was the latter, because he never even mentioned his slip of the tongue. He was all business, his demeanour as cold and demanding as it had been at their first meeting. Last night might never have existed for him.

If only she could dismiss it so successfully. But, as he alternately ordered and coaxed her into the poses he required, she couldn't help recalling those moments in his pool. He had been another person then, loving and giving, instead of autocratic as he was now. She wondered if he even remembered calling her Trina last night.

As it turned out, he did remember. When they had finished the shots and he suggested adjourning to the pub next door to celebrate, she explained why she couldn't, adding that she needed time to pack and prepare.

'Is that the only reason, or is there something else?'

'I can't imagine what you mean,' she said sarcastically.

'Yes, you can. You're different today, somehow.'

'No, I'm not. I'm me—Danni—in case you'd forgotten.'

His gaze was level. 'I hadn't forgotten.'

'You did last night,' she reminded him.

His eyes darkened and his brows drew together. 'So that's what all this is about. You're sulking because I called you Trina in the heat of the moment. But I was under a lot of pressure. There's no need for you to go running off to the country over it.'

'I'm not running off,' she snapped back, keeping her fists clenched to keep from lashing out at him. He still couldn't see that this was important to her.

'Last night, you had to put your work first. Now I'm doing the same. You made more than one mistake by calling me Trina last night. You also assumed that I'd behave the same way she would, accepting a back seat whenever it suits you. Well, I don't intend to. Yesterday was some sort of... of aberration. I wasn't thinking clearly. But I am now, and it's time I returned to my own life, instead of swanning around like a pale imitation of my sister.'

Leaving him staring after her, she slammed the studio door and hurtled down the stairs two at a time, astonished at the ferocity of her outburst. It was just as well that she was getting away from Rowan. Around him, she felt as if she was riding an emotional roller-coaster!

At home that evening, she tried to tell herself she had done the right thing by walking out on Rowan. He had shown no regard for her feelings. Hadn't he proved it by his behaviour at his penthouse, and now at his studio? She was well rid of him, before she got more involved.

Except that she was *already* involved, she realised with a shock. That was why his indifference was so painful. If he meant nothing to her, why should she care what he called her?

She was still trying to convince herself she was doing the right thing when she walked out of Ray's office next morning with a folder crammed with background about the small wineries of the Hunter Valley. One of them, Bedales, would be her base while she researched her story.

Ordinarily, she would have been elated at receiving such a choice assignment, if only she hadn't been achingly aware that every mile she drove away from Sydney increased the distance between herself and Rowan. Was he missing her, or had he already replaced her with one of his model friends? That he was much more likely to be closeted in his darkroom, rushing out the replacement cover shots, gave her some comfort. Her own ambivalence made her smile. It was all right for her to welcome this break from him, as long as he didn't feel the same way.

The shadows were lengthening by the time she reached the Hunter Valley region. Bedales was located a few miles inland from the industrial city of Cessnock, in the foothills of the Mount View Ranges. On either side of her, the vines were just reaching their peak—richly leafed and laden with clustered grapes.

As she crested a rise and came upon a cluster of buildings, she gave a sigh of appreciation. The winery was built of convict-quarried stone, with a wide post-and-rail veranda on three sides. Although it looked historic, Danni recalled from her briefing with Ray that the winery was fairly young. The owner's choice of old building materials made it look a century older than its years.

'G'day. You must be Danni O'Dare. I've been looking out for your car.' The effusive greeting met her almost before she had finished parking her car outside the main building.

She climbed out to be met by a slightly rotund man, shorter than her, with sandy hair brushed across his forehead, unsuccessfully disguising a bare patch of scalp. His smile was so warm and irresistible that she found herself smiling back. 'Hello, Mr...Bedford, isn't it?'

'Laurie, please,' he asserted. 'We don't stand on ceremony around here.'

'And I'm Danni,' she reciprocated, warming to him already. He was obviously so pleased to have her here that it took away just a little of the sting of Rowan's unfeeling attitude. At least with Laurie Bedford, there was no confusion as to who she was, she thought ruefully.

It was her role as a reporter for an influential publication which influenced him, she reminded herself. At the same time, she got the impression that Laurie Bedford found her attractive. After the last few days with Rowan, it was a relief to be the object of a man's frank admiration, even if the man wasn't the one dominating her thoughts. Steady, girl, she told herself shakily. She had taken this assignment so she could have some time to think, not to create fresh complications.

Laurie took her suitcase from her, hefting it in one hand as if it weighed nothing. 'I've put you and your photographer together in one of our guest cabins,' he explained. 'I hope you don't mind sharing, but we don't have much accommodation here, and we're fully booked at the moment.'

'It's quite all right, we're old friends,' she said, and quickened her steps to keep up with Laurie, who was already forging across the expanse of lawn which separated the winery from a small group of cabins.

Reaching them, Laurie flung open the door of the nearest one. 'I hope you'll be comfortable here, Danni. At least you have the place to yourself for the first night. I understand that your photographer isn't arriving until tomorrow.'

'So my editor tells me.' She caught her breath as she looked inside the cabin. 'This is charming.'

Inside, the log walls had been left natural, while the tallow-wood floor was polished to a warm patina. Off the combined living area and dining-room was a tiny kitchen, made cosily cheerful with curtains and tablecloth of red and white gingham. To her right, a pair of doors led to what must be bedrooms, with a bathroom separating them. 'There's plenty of room for two,' she assured Laurie. 'I can type my notes up on the table, and we'll have a bedroom each. What more could we need?'

He seemed relieved and pleased with her approval. 'In that case, I'll leave you to unpack.' But he made no move to go, and shifted his weight from one foot to the other, as if there was something on his mind.

'Is there anything else I should know?' she asked.

'Well,' he took a deep breath and went on in a rush, 'I've stocked the kitchen with food, but you may not want to cook on your first night here, so I was hoping you'd join me in the restaurant for dinner.' He pointed to a vast building, shaped like a wine barrel tipped on its side. 'The restaurant is part of our tasting cellar, and it's really quite unusual.'

If only it was Rowan asking her, she thought, with a flood of such intense longing for him that she was shaken. She felt like collapsing at the kitchen table, resting her head on her hands and weeping from sheer loneliness and heartache. With a tremendous effort, she managed to smile at Laurie, who was watching her expectantly. 'Your restaurant looks enchanting, and I must try it while I'm here. We might even take some pictures there for the story. But I'm rather tired after the drive down, so I think I'll have an early night. Thanks for the invitation. It was very kind.'

His look told her the invitation hadn't been prompted out of kindness. 'I understand,' he said, disappointment in his voice. 'But if you should change your mind, you're welcome to join me for a nightcap later. I don't usually go to bed until after eleven, with all the paperwork for the winery. So if you have trouble sleeping, or get lonely or anything...' He let his voice trail off.

Because he seemed to expect some sort of response, she shook hands with him awkwardly, then he left her alone to explore the cabin. There were two bedrooms, a single and a double, and she left the larger room for Donna Healey, so she would have somewhere to stow her photographic equipment.

Laurie's attentiveness had only reminded her of how far away she was from Rowan. What was he doing now? Getting ready to go out for the evening? It was painful even to think about, and yet she couldn't blame him if he did. He didn't know whether she intended to come back. How could he, when she didn't know herself?

She tried to tell herself he had left her no choice, but somehow the argument sounded hollow. Couldn't they have talked, reached an understanding? Couldn't she have given just a little more?

No, lovers didn't call each other by the wrong names. Even so, she couldn't dispel the memory of the intimacy they had shared. Rowan's kisses, Rowan's touch, Rowan's lovemaking, they were all imprinted in her memory as surely as if he had etched them there in flame.

'Damn, damn, damn!' she muttered. Was he going to follow her everywhere she travelled? For he was here, as surely as if it had been in the flesh. She stirred restlessly, shedding clothes as she moved around the cabin. What sort of a job could she do if she turned down every dinner invitation because it didn't come from Rowan? She had gathered some of her best story material in the relaxed atmosphere of a restaurant. Was that avenue now closed to her as well?

As well as what? She came to a halt in front of a timber-framed mirror which reflected her shocked expression. As well as love, she realised. Could there ever be any other man for her after Rowan?

Was he thinking of her right now? Oh, God, she hoped he was, because it might mean there was some hope for them. Maybe while she was here, he might realise he needed her as much as she accepted now, she needed him. Dressed only in her underslip, she hugged her arms around herself in pale imitation of his embrace, and throbbing heat pulsated through her.

How could anything as foolish as a slip of the tongue be allowed to come between them? Why couldn't she see that in Sydney, before she was crazy enough to leave him?

Two quick strides brought her to the telephone. With fingers made clumsy by haste, she dialled the Sydney code then Rowan's studio, sure he would be working on the last of the swimwear shots.

Knowing that the phone was ringing in his studio made her feel close to him even before the phone was answered. 'Hello? Rowan Traynor Photography.'

The fire in her veins turned to ice as she recognised the woman's voice. Somehow, she made her vocal cords co-operate. 'Trina, it's me, Danni.'

There was a pause. 'Oh, hi, Danni. Where are you calling from?'

'I'm in the Hunter Valley. I gather you got my message on your answering machine?' And knew just what to do about it, an inner voice added bitterly.

'That's right. I only got back from the Gold Coast this morning.'

She had no patience for Trina's small talk. 'Is Rowan there? Let me talk to him.' Let him make it all right, she prayed inwardly.

'I'm afraid he's in the darkroom. He won't be much longer because we're going out to dinner. After my long trip, I'm starving. Did you want me to give him a message?'

Danni thought furiously, but could think of nothing she wanted to say. It hadn't taken Rowan long to find the most convenient substitute for Danni, but she couldn't say that in a message, so she said her goodbyes and hung up.

What a fool she had nearly made of herself. She had intended to tell Rowan that she had been wrong to risk what they had over a stupid mistake. Now she knew that the mistake was in trusting herself to him in the first place. Even though he recognised the flaws in Trina's character, he had wasted no time teaming up with her once Danni was out of the way.

Forbidding herself to think, she went through the motions of unpacking, then wandered around the small kitchen, picking at some fruit and cheese Laurie had left there. She had no appetite and no enthusiasm for anything. There was only a crushing emptiness inside her, as if all her vitality had been drained away.

Unbidden, Laurie's words came into her mind: 'If you get lonely or can't sleep...'

Mechanically, she lifted the phone again and dialled Laurie's extension at the main house. When he answered, she forced a smile into her voice, although her brain felt like ice. 'Hello, Laurie. It's Danni. If the offer is still open, I've decided I would like that nightcap, after all.'

CHAPTER EIGHT

'JUST how serious is this commitment of yours?' Laurie asked her as they began their tour of the winery next morning.

He had every right to ask, she conceded. She had been willing enough to seek his company last night. She hadn't told him about Rowan's duplicity, but Laurie had somehow understood her need for companionship, and had provided it without expecting anything in return. Most men would have drawn their own conclusions, had she arrived on their doorstep late at night. But Laurie, bless him, wasn't most men.

'I don't know,' she answered truthfully. 'Until last night, I would have said it was very serious. Now—I'm not so sure any more.'

'Ah, after last night,' he said sagely.

She touched his arm gently. 'I really enjoyed your company last night, honestly. I wasn't just using you.' She stumbled slightly over the last part, not sure herself if it was entirely the truth.

He guessed as much. 'I invited you over. Whatever your reasons for accepting, I'm glad you came.'

She was glad, too, in her own way. Her mind had been in such turmoil after her phone call to Rowan that she hadn't known which way to turn. But for Laurie's kindness, she might have jumped into her car and driven all the way back to Sydney to confront Rowan and Trina.

Which wasn't the way, she saw now in daylight. Just because they had made love, she didn't have any claim on him, as Trina's presence in his studio had reminded her. So why did she feel so wretched when she thought of them together last night?

Something Laurie was saying wrenched her back to the present. 'I'm sorry,' she said, afraid she had missed something important. 'You did say you were growing white wine grapes on red grape vines?'

Laurie laughed, but carefully explained the process again for her. Watching her write furiously in her notebook, he became thoughtful. 'It's fun showing you my work, Danni.' He toyed with the curling tendril of a vine. 'I suppose it's just your training. You can't really find all this as fascinating as you pretend.'

'It isn't pretence. My interest *is* professional, but your love of this place is infectious.'

'Is it? Then maybe you'd consider coming back here after you finish the story. I've been wanting to get someone to write the history of Bedales. The grant on this property dates back to 1864, when wine grapes were first planted here. The slab hut built by the first settlers is still standing. I'd love to show it to you.'

She knew what he was proposing—that she put their association on a more personal footing—and for a moment she was tempted. Laurie was easy to like, and he made no secret of his liking for her. But she knew instinctively that she could never feel anything stronger than liking for him, and it wasn't fair to give him false hopes. 'I'd like to come back for a visit one day,' she said, her tone gentle. 'But it will depend on my commitments.' Deliberately, she used his expression.

He brushed the fine strands of hair away from his forehead. 'I understand. I can't pretend I like it, but I do understand. All the same, I'm quite serious about the book, and I think you're the perfect person to write it.'

She felt her face growing warm. 'You're very kind, Laurie, considering you know so little about my work.'

His eyes darkened with unmistakable emotion. 'It wasn't entirely your work I was thinking of. You fit in so well here, Danni. Working with you on the book would be very special.'

The proposal needed a lot of thought, she knew. Laurie was pleasant company and she was enjoying her visit to the wine country. She could also use the book commission, she acknowledged a little ruefully. But she didn't need the complications which were bound to go with the job. But that was her problem, not Laurie's, and he had paid her a great compliment with his offer.

Impulsively, she leaned across the staked vines and planted a light kiss of appreciation on his cheek. 'You're a dear, Laurie.'

The look he gave her was full of speculation, but he said nothing.

The rest of the day passed in a blur of activity, as Laurie showed her around the rest of the vineyard, ending with a tour of the winery itself. By the time they reached the tasting-room, her notebook was filled with the details she would need to write her articles.

'But you still have to sample the finished product,' Laurie told her. She watched curiously as he tapped a container and siphoned off a glass of ruby-coloured liquid. 'This wine has been developing for nine months already,' he said, holding it up to the light. 'It's going to make a wonderful port.'

He led her from cask to cask around the immense sale-room, showing her how to taste the different wines. Soon her nostrils were filled with the sweet-sour smell which hung in the musty air, and her throat was dry from the ritual of sniffing, tasting and rinsing wine.

'I thought wine-tasters had an enviable job. Now I'm not so sure,' she told Laurie, pulling a wry face.

'It's like mattress-testing—a myth,' he agreed. 'But since you've been such a splendid student, we'll sample one more wine properly.' He handed her a glass of golden straw-coloured wine which he explained was a 1978 Bedford Riesling.

She sipped it and smiled in appreciation. 'I suppose I should tell you how soft, elegant and full-flavoured it is, but I only know I like it,' she confessed.

His eyes held a golden glint which echoed the colour of the wine, as he regarded her. 'There's no harm in knowing what you like.'

She set her glass down. 'Laurie, I . . .'

'Please don't spoil what has been, up to now, one of my favourite days,' he interrupted. 'I know

there can't be any repeats but, like a good wine,
I'd like to savour this one while it lasts.'

He refilled their glasses, and she raised hers in a
toast. 'To my host.'

He returned the gesture. 'To my beautiful guest.'
A pang pierced her. Why couldn't she fall in love
with Laurie Bedford? Everything would be so
simple. He liked and admired her, and she liked
him back. He didn't even know her twin, so there
could be no suggestion that he saw anyone else when
he looked at her. And Bedales was one of the most
magical places she could imagine living in. Yes, it
would be simple. But it would never be enough.

Perhaps it was the heady effect of the wine, but
she found herself agreeing to have dinner with
Laurie at a restaurant in Cessnock. She told herself
she wasn't harming anyone by agreeing, least of all
Laurie, who knew how she felt about him. At the
same time, she faced the fact that she was only
going out with him to avoid being alone with her
thoughts.

He agreed to collect her at eight-thirty for the
drive to Cessnock. This would give her time to type
up her notes and map out her articles, then prepare
for the evening.

To her surprise, there was no sign of Donna
Healey when she reached the cabin. Surely the photographer should be here by now? If she hadn't
known how capable and resourceful Donna was,
she would have begun to worry. But, if anything
had gone wrong, she would have telephoned, she
reasoned. Maybe Donna had been late leaving

Sydney and would turn up while Danni was out at dinner with Laurie.

Who was Rowan with tonight? The thought forced its way into her mind. What was he doing right now? Certainly not missing her. Any such notion had been destroyed when her twin answered the phone last night.

'Stop it!' she muttered aloud. Flying to her type-writer, she jammed a sheet of paper into it and began to type furiously, blinking back the tears which threatened to splash on to the paper. Work was the answer. Work was the way to get Rowan out of her mind so she could go on living without him, as she must.

Gradually, the discipline of her craft overtook her, and she became immersed in her task. It was almost eight by the time she looked up, her eyes heavy and red with fatigue. But the article was almost finished. It would need polishing, of course, but the shape and substance were there.

She smiled wryly to herself. Thoughts of Rowan might torment her, but they also drove her to do her best work.

The restaurant Laurie chose was rustic in appearance, but comfortable and efficiently run. The furniture seemed to be carved out of split logs.

'I enjoyed today,' she told Laurie as they studied the menu.

'You've timed your visit well. If you'd arrived at vintage time in February, we'd be working around the clock.'

His look said he would have found time for her somehow, and her discomfort returned. What was she doing here, when the only man she wanted to be with was hundreds of miles away? She realised that Laurie had asked her a question. 'I'm sorry?'

'I asked if you'd prefer me to order for you?'

She would have preferred to forget dinner and escape to her cabin to think, but she knew Laurie would be disappointed. He wasn't to blame for her confused state of mind, and she didn't want him to think he was. 'That's fine with me,' she agreed.

As it turned out, his choices were excellent, and she soon rediscovered her appetite as the courses were set in front of her. They started with a carrot and orange soup, followed by a veal and peppercorn terrine, served with a selection of Bedales' own wines. During the meal, Laurie drew her out so artfully that, by the time the meal ended, she had told him much more than she intended to about herself. She realised that they had talked hardly at all about him, although she now knew that he was a former lawyer who had given up a successful practice after visiting the Hunter region on holiday and falling in love with the area.

'Were you a born writer?' he asked, once more turning the conversation back to her.

'I've always loved to write,' she confirmed. 'I chose journalism as the best way to make my living with a typewriter.'

'Does your twin share your talent?'

She shook her head. 'She has no interest in writing. She never cared for books and study, so her choice of modelling was probably the right one. She's much better at making the most of her looks—quite a beauty, in fact.'

He frowned. 'You say she's the beauty of the family, yet you're identical twins. Are you sure you aren't selling yourself short?'

He had already made it clear that he was attracted to her, so he would think so, but she had to disillusion him. 'We are alike in looks, but Trina has the kind of inner glow which makes her appear more beautiful. She's also good with make-up and fashion, while I just don't have the interest.'

'All the same, I think you're wrong about yourself.' His voice dropped and his hand slid across the table until their fingers touched. 'I think you're beautiful, Danni. The fact that you don't seem to think so only makes you more attractive to me.'

'It's kind of you to say so, but . . .'

'No buts,' he said firmly. 'Whatever gave you the idea that you're not beautiful?'

Because of the boyfriends she had lost to Trina, she thought ruefully. Because of Keith Bowden, the first man she had been ready to love, who had preferred Trina over Danni and made no secret of it. Oh, she'd had plenty of lessons.

It hurt to think that Rowan might be the latest of those lessons. 'Let's not talk about me any more,' she urged. 'I'd like to know more about your winery for my story.'

'Only the winery and the story?' he asked sadly.

'I'm afraid so. I like you, Laurie, truly, but as I told you last night, I'm already committed.' However one-sided it may be, she added to herself.

'I should have known I don't have that kind of luck,' he said, trying to sound cheerful and failing.

She touched his hand. 'I'm sorry, but I can't let you go on thinking...'

'...just what I was thinking,' he finished for her. 'I appreciate your honesty, Danni, but I enjoyed my thoughts while they lasted.'

The waiter brought their coffee and she sipped it pensively. 'Have you never married, Laurie?'

'I came close once,' he admitted. 'But she was on the rebound. Sooner or later she would have regretted it and started to hate me.'

'No one could hate you, Laurie,' Danni reassured him.

His generous mouth twisted into a grimace. 'Maybe not. It's the loving that seems to cause all the trouble.'

How right he was, she reflected. 'I wonder if it's worth it,' she speculated.

He gestured for their bill before answering. 'I'll let you know when I find out.'

They drove back to Bedales mostly in silence, punctuated by occasional small talk. Realising the depth of Laurie's feelings for her, Danni felt sorry that she had allowed him to take her out. It was only making things harder for both of them. After tonight, there would be no repetition, she promised herself. Laurie deserved better treatment. However she dressed it up, she was using him, and she suspected he realised it too.

When he helped her out of the car outside her cabin, his mood was sad and withdrawn. She longed to say something to reassure him, but could think of nothing which wouldn't make the situation harder than it was. She settled for, 'Thank you, I've had a lovely evening.'

He opened her cabin door and stood back to let her enter. 'I'm glad. I've enjoyed your company, too.'

In the narrow doorway, his face was close to hers and, as he leaned closer, she realised he meant to kiss her.

Panic assailed her. This wasn't how she wanted the evening to end at all.

She was saved from the necessity to respond by the sound of the shower splashing in the bathroom. Looking around, she noticed a pile of photographic equipment in the centre of the living-room. 'Donna must have arrived while we were out,' she said weakly.

With her comment, Laurie emerged from his trancelike state. 'Yes, it looks like it. I'd better say goodnight, then.'

Before she could move, he grasped her upper arms in an irresistible grip and leaned forward, touching his mouth to hers. Then he released her with a groan of self-recrimination. His expression was anguished as he turned away from her. As he walked quickly back towards the main building, she saw that his hands were clenched into fists.

'Very touching,' came a voice behind her.

She whirled, every nerve-ending springing to quivering life. 'Rowan! What are you doing here?'

He stood framed in the bathroom door, his magnificent body covered only by a towel, wrapped carelessly around his mid-section. His torso was bare and glistened from his shower, the chest hairs lying sleek and dark against his skin. His muscular legs were planted wide apart, and his feet were bare. 'I came to see you. Apparently, I had no need to rush, after all.'

'It wasn't what you think,' she said tautly, then wondered why she was bothering to reassure him. He was the one with some explaining to do, not her.

'Of course it wasn't, but it would have been if you'd had the cabin to yourself.'

Anger flared in her. 'You have no right to judge me,' she flung at him. 'What I do is none of your business.'

'Because I called you by the wrong name in the heat of a moment?'

'No! That was only part of it.'

He folded his arms across his broad chest and levelled a searching gaze at her. 'Go ahead, I'm listening.'

This was absurd! How could she possibly explain her fears to him with any measure of dignity, when he was watching her like this? 'Can't you get dressed first?' she demanded.

His look changed to one of satisfaction. 'You can't be as indifferent to me as you pretend, or my state of undress wouldn't bother you,' he observed.

She felt the colour flooding into her face and looked away before he could see it. 'It doesn't bother me. What bothers me is why you turned up in my cabin, unannounced, in the middle of the night.'

'But it's my cabin, too,' he said, sounding surprised that she should even question his presence.

'When I checked in, the receptionist assured me you didn't mind sharing. Apparently you told her we're old friends.'

Horrified, she stared at him. 'But I was expecting Donna Healey.'

'You said your photographer. The receptionist didn't seem to know who you were expecting.'

Oh, God, he was right. She had told the woman to put the photographer in her cabin, without specifying any name—or sex. 'But you can't stay here,' she insisted. 'What about Donna? Where will she sleep?'

'In Honolulu, I expect,' was his calm reply. 'You see, we switched assignments. Right now, she's on her way to Hawaii to photograph volcanoes.'

'You're taking her place?' He nodded, and despair gripped her. She shook her head violently. 'This isn't a good idea.'

'Don't you trust me to do a good job?'

'Don't be ridiculous!' If anything, he was over-qualified for such a simple assignment. Photographing volcanoes in Hawaii was much more worthy of his skills and talent.

'Then what's the problem?'

He was being deliberately obtuse. 'I came up here to get away from you,' she said carefully. 'I thought we meant something to each other, then, after you mistook me for Trina, I needed some time to think things over. As it turned out, I was right. You are fickle. As long as there's a woman in your bed, you don't care who she is.'

'So you did speak to Trina last night. I thought I heard the phone ring while I was in the darkroom, but she told me it was a wrong number.'

'You're telling me!'

'Stop it, Danni,' he ordered, his voice harsh. 'I guessed it was you much later, and I also guessed what sort of interpretation you would put on the call. It seems I was right.'

'Are you surprised? It didn't take you two long to get back together,' she said bitterly.

'We aren't back together,' he snapped. 'She had a fight with Malcolm or whatever his name is, and came around to the studio to cry on my shoulder.'

His shoulders were more than broad enough, she observed unhappily. Wearing only a towel, he looked like a modern gladiator, and it was an effort to stop her eyes following the dark line of hair which plunged beneath the towel.

To distract herself, she went into the kitchen and set about making two mugs of coffee. The mechanical task kept her hands occupied, although her mind persisted in dwelling on the man standing close behind her. 'What you do is no concern of mine,' she said over her shoulder.

He moved closer, until she could feel the heat radiating from his shower-warmed body. 'Are you sure about that?'

'Of course I'm sure.' She turned, intending to hand him the coffee, but he was standing right behind her, and she came up hard against his muscular torso. With a coffee-cup in each hand, she had no way of fending him off, and his arms went around her.

When he pulled her against him, she almost spilled the coffee, and had to set it down on the countertop behind him. 'Don't,' she said feebly.

Her protest carried no conviction, and was soon smothered in his kiss. Although he had hardly been out of her thoughts all day, she was unprepared for the assault his physical presence made on her senses. She felt herself turning to jelly as his kisses trailed up and down her throat, and his hands grew warm against the small of her back.

'I've missed you so much,' he said into the hair at the nape of her neck. 'I had to see you again. I thought, if we worked together, on your turf this time, maybe we could work things out.'

'Then you and Trina didn't . . .'

'No, we didn't,' he said firmly, meeting her eyes. 'Any more than you and Bedford did.'

'Then you believe me?'

'Shouldn't I?'

'Yes. Laurie's attracted to me, but it wouldn't be fair to lead him on . . .'

She paused, and his eyes glinted with interest. 'When you already belong to me, is that what you were going to say?'

How could it be, when she didn't know herself what she meant to him? 'Is that how things are?' she asked huskily.

'If it's what you want.'

Was it what she wanted? Could she give herself to him whole-heartedly, when she still harboured doubts about the rightness of their relationship?

'I'm waiting,' he persisted.

'Yes, it's what I want.' God help her, it was the only thing she wanted, to be his wholly and completely, in body and mind. Nothing else seemed to matter any more.

He let out the breath he'd been holding, and it dawned on her that he hadn't been sure of her answer at all.

'Thank God,' he said raggedly.

Putting his arm around her shoulders, he drew her closer, so she could feel his shower-warmed body radiating heat through her clothes. Her pulses began to beat their now-familiar tattoo, which signalled his nearness, and it was an effort to breathe normally.

In a trance, she felt herself walking beside him until they reached the bedroom next to hers, where she saw that Rowan had unpacked his things. Then he urged her down on to the edge of the bed, and took his place beside her. All the while, his eyes never left her face. 'I've missed you so much,' he said fiercely, and leaned closer.

She nodded as the ache inside her swelled until it threatened to choke her. 'Me, too,' she admitted in a husky whisper.

With a groan of defeat, he clasped her to him and his lips began to rove through her hair as he murmured sweet, meaningless phrases deep in his throat.

How could she have ever doubted him? she wondered as every part of her responded to his touch. To remind herself that he was really here, she sent her own hands on a voyage of exploration, and heard his indrawn breath as her fingers curled into the coarse hair on his chest. Gently, he urged her back against the pillows and rested on his elbows above her, his expression tender as he cupped her head and bent his mouth to kiss her again. Wildfire tore along her veins and she arched her body to meet him, knowing only he could quench the inferno inside her.

Their joining was like the headlong rush down a mountain after the laborious climb to the top. At the end of it, they were both exhausted but exhilarated. Rowan propped himself up on one elbow and looked down at her, his eyes warm. 'Now are you glad I came?'

'I was glad the moment I turned and saw you standing in the doorway,' she admitted, the need for any pretence completely gone.

He feigned annoyance. 'You mean, you let me go through hell to prove my point, when you were already convinced?'

Reaching up, she smoothed away the fierce frown with a finger. 'Maybe I like being convinced.'

'You're a witch, Danni O'Dare,' he growled. 'But if convincing is what you need...'

And he proceeded to give her another lesson.

Much later, he padded through to the kitchen and found a bottle of champagne Laurie had placed in the refrigerator for them, and returned with two brimming glasses. He handed one to her. 'A nightcap for milady.'

'I don't think I need one any more. I'm going to sleep like a baby.' She scrambled up and swung her legs over the side of the bed. 'I'd better go back to my own bed if I'm to be fit for anything in the morning.'

'You're in your own bed,' he said severely. 'From now on, my bed is yours. I thought I had convinced you of that.'

In mock alarm, she backed away, coming up against the headboard of the bed. 'I'm convinced! Don't beat me!'

'Beat you?' he laughed. 'Now, there's an idea.'

'I knew I would have been safer if Donna had been here.'

He regarded her seriously. 'Are you still annoyed because I changed places with her?'

'I was never really annoyed. You just caught me by surprise,' she admitted. 'Ever since last night, you've been on my mind. So I could hardly believe you were really here. I...I wasn't even sure I wanted you to be.'

'And now?'

'Now I'm sure. When I got Trina on the phone, I admit I didn't know what to think. It was as if my worst fears were being realised.'

He frowned in self-condemnation. 'I understand that now, and I could kick myself for taking it so lightly. You tried to tell me you were sensitive to that particular issue, and I was a boor to let it happen. It wasn't until you'd left Sydney that I saw how unimportant a few rolls of film were compared with the way I felt about you. Yet I'd put my worries about work ahead of your feelings. Can you forgive me?'

She leaned over and kissed him lightly. 'All the way up here, I told myself I was an idiot for risking what we could have over such a trifling issue.'

'It wasn't a trifle to you.'

He wandered over to the window and stood gazing out over the rolling hills, which were silhouetted in the moonlight and spangled by more stars than Danni had known existed. Then he turned back to her. 'Learning to trust is the very devil, isn't it?'

CHAPTER NINE

NEXT morning, Danni was awakened by the clattering of dishes in the kitchen. It took her a few minutes to recall who could be in the other room, then she felt her colour heighten. Rowan was here, and they had spent the night together.

She started as he came in carrying a steaming cup of coffee. 'Good, you're awake.'

'Why didn't you wake me?' she asked a little shyly, all too conscious of the crumpled state of the other half of the bed.

'You looked too beautiful in sleep. I hadn't the heart to disturb you.'

'All the same, I should be up. Laurie wants to show me the winemaking process this morning.' As soon as she mentioned Laurie, a shadow flickered across Rowan's eyes. She knew he was remembering the way Laurie had kissed her last night. But at least Rowan knew why it had happened. She still had to face Laurie and apologise to him, although she wasn't looking forward to the idea.

'Does Bedford know I'm here?' Rowan asked tautly.

She shook her head. 'We were both expecting Donna Healey. But it shouldn't make any difference to Laurie whether the photographer is a man or a woman.'

'From the interest he was showing in you, I'd say it will make all the difference,' he observed. Before she could reply, he started towards the door, then paused. 'I hope an omelette suits you for breakfast. I found eggs and milk in the refrigerator.'

Although she protested that she wasn't hungry, when she joined him in the kitchen, her nostrils were tantalised by the smell of herbed omelette simmering in a pan. Rowan was squeezing oranges into juice as she approached, and she began to wish that she had asked for breakfast, after all.

She looked surprised when he slid a plate of golden omelette in front of her, and set a glass of juice beside it. 'How did you know I would change my mind?' she asked.

He grinned. 'You're forgetting how well I know you, Danni. I also know what country air can do to one's appetite. So eat up. We have work to do.'

As she'd expected, Laurie was waiting for them at the entrance to the winery. Deliberately, Danni had gone ahead of Rowan while the photographer readied his gear. She was determined to sort things out with Laurie before Rowan appeared on the scene.

'About last night; I want you to know I had a lovely evening,' she began.

'Until I blew it on the cabin doorstep,' he said ruefully.

'No, you didn't. It was my fault,' she insisted. 'I knew how you felt. I shouldn't have agreed to go.'

He smiled sadly. 'Whatever you do, don't apologise for giving me an evening in your company. That would be like asking for the return of a gift.'

Embarrassed, she turned away and almost collided with Rowan, coming to join them. Laurie's eyebrows arched questioningly when he saw the other man. 'This is Rowan Traynor. Donna Healey was called to another assignment,' she explained haltingly, knowing the tremor in her voice betrayed her feelings about Rowan. But Laurie merely offered Rowan his hand unhesitatingly. 'Welcome to Bedales. It was good you could step in at short notice.'

'I was glad to do it,' Rowan said with a warm glance in Danni's direction.

As she coloured, Laurie's eyes followed her. His look plainly said, 'So this is your commitment.' Lines of pain were etched on his face, and Danni wished there had been some other way for him to find out. Her own experiences told her only too well how painful it was to love someone who didn't return the feeling.

She quickened her steps towards the main building, and yelped as Laurie's fingers dug into her arm. She was yanked backwards, almost off her feet. Suddenly her ears were filled with a roaring sound, and a huge tractor loomed alongside her, towing a lawn-mowing contraption in its wake. The driver, his hearing muffled by ear protectors, hadn't heard them as he'd emerged from behind the cabins.

The sound died away as he rounded the main building, and Danni gave Laurie a shaky smile of gratitude. 'Thanks. I almost walked under that monster.'

'Fool driver should have watched where he was going,' Laurie fumed, obviously as shaken as she was. 'He's new, but he should know better than to work near the cabins without keeping a sharp lookout. I've a good mind to send him packing.'

'No, please,' Danni pleaded, not wanting the man to lose his job because of her. 'It wasn't entirely his fault. I wasn't looking where I was going.'

Laurie accepted her assurance reluctantly. 'I won't fire him if you'd rather I didn't. But I will warn him about such idiotic behaviour.'

Relieved, Danni nodded. She looked around furtively, and was relieved to find that Rowan was preoccupied with photographing the verdant hills with their soldierly rows of vines. If he had seen her near-miss, she felt sure he would have hauled the errant driver down from his cab and taught him a lesson on the spot. She shuddered at the idea, then lowered her eyes warningly at Laurie as Rowan rejoined them, saying loudly, 'I can't wait to see the actual winemaking process.'

Taking his cue from her, Laurie squared his shoulders with an obvious effort and addressed them both. 'You won't see much at this time of year. There are no grapes going through, but you can follow the path they normally take through to bottling.'

As they entered the building, Danni's first impression was of a number of huge stainless steel tanks and a network of pipes. Laurie gestured towards the equipment. 'All this is used at the start of the winemaking process. The crushed grapes are fermented here, then stored in other steel tanks until bottling.'

Danni felt a stab of disappointment. 'It isn't very romantic, is it?'

'You'll feel happier when we reach the section with the oak casks and barrels,' Laurie told her. He stepped forward, and seemed about to place an arm around her shoulder to lead her on, then thought better of it and gestured in the air. 'We go this way.'

Behind them, Danni heard Rowan's growl of disapproval and tensed. This morning, there was no mistaking his air of possessiveness towards her. Seeing how he eyed Laurie warily, she wondered how she could have thought Rowan was indifferent to her. If the intimacy of last night hadn't convinced her beyond any doubt, his behaviour today would have.

With an effort, she concentrated on taking notes as they continued their tour. 'During the year, we make hundreds of decisions which affect the wine,' Laurie explained. 'We have to decide how little or how much to prune the vines, whether or not to fertilise them, and when. As vintage time approaches, we constantly check the sugar and acid levels of the grapes, so they can be picked on exactly the right day.'

'The exact day?' she echoed. 'Is it as precise as that?'

'It is, I'm afraid. Picking the grapes a day too early or too late will affect the quality of the wine. And those are just the decisions we need to make before the grapes are brought in here for fermentation. There are just as many details to be juggled afterwards.'

'So winemaking isn't the leisurely process I imagined,' she remarked. 'It calls for one decision after another.'

'Life's like that,' Rowan cut in, surprising her.

She jumped slightly. In order to concentrate on her work, she had pretended that he wasn't trailing after them, his camera working furiously. Now she was reminded as he climbed agilely up on to a row of pipes to snap the winery from an unusual angle, one of the qualities for which he was famous. Suddenly he aimed the camera at her and she heard the motor whirr as he took the shot.

She ducked her head in embarrassment. 'There's no need to take any shots of me.'

The warmth in his gaze was unmistakably possessive. 'That was for my private collection.'

The last shot he'd taken of her for his collection had been at the topless section of beach at Bondi, she recalled, and was sure he'd meant to remind her of it.

Uncomfortably, she glanced at Laurie, but he was ostentatiously studying some piece of equipment. She felt a flash of anger at Rowan. He knew how Laurie felt about her, and also that she'd made the situation clear to the winemaker. There was no need for Rowan to remind him of his place at every opportunity.

When they were alone in the cabin a short time later, she wasted no time in venting her annoyance.

'Poor Laurie didn't know where to put himself,' she said crossly.

In the act of reloading his camera with film, Rowan froze. 'So it's "poor Laurie" now, is it? I thought you said he didn't mean anything to you?'

'And he doesn't,' she snapped back. 'But there's nothing wrong with showing a little courtesy.'

'Not to any man who looks at you the way he does,' Rowan grumbled.

'Stop this!' she commanded. 'I've already told you how I feel about you, and shown you in every way I can. I won't be wrapped in cotton wool and hidden away from the world, to be brought out for your private amusement.'

Rowan stared at her in astonishment. 'Is that what I was doing?'

'That's what it felt like.'

'Oh, hell!' He dragged his fingers through his hair, tousling it. 'I didn't mean to be so possessive. I suppose I was a bit hard on Bedford, wasn't I?'

She refused to be deceived by his apparent capitulation. 'Yes, you were,' she agreed. 'And I understand why you feel that way. But I'm not your mother, and you'll simply have to accept my word that there's no other man in my life but you.' Nor could there be, she thought, but kept the words to herself. Rowan had to find it out for himself.

He swung a chair around and straddled it, regarding her thoughtfully. 'I still have a long way to go, don't I?'

'We both do. What we have in bed together...' the words caught in her throat but she forced them out '...is just the beginning of what we could have.'

'But it isn't enough?' he second-guessed her.

'You know it isn't. For me, a successful relationship has to be built on kindness, caring and trust, as much as good sex.'

He nodded, his eyes dark. 'You're right. But then, I haven't had much experience of the kind of relationship you're describing.'

'Never?' she probed.

He concentrated, remembering. 'Things were different when I was very young. My mother hadn't tired of marriage then, and motherhood was still a novelty.' His expression softened. 'I suppose it was pretty good then.'

'Do you remember when things began to change?'

'When Dad started accepting assignments away from home. He'd given up his work as a war correspondent, of course, but he still liked to travel when he could.'

'You don't think that had anything to do with your mother's behaviour, do you?' she suggested.

He seemed to resist allocating any of the blame to the father he had hero-worshipped as a boy. 'Why should it? I told you, he spent as much time with me as he could.'

'With you. What about with your mother?'

'All right, so she was lonely. Are you trying to tell me that gives a woman the right to abandon her marriage vows?'

'Of course I'm not. I'm only suggesting a reason why she might have acted as she did. It doesn't mean every woman is going to do the same thing.'

'So I shouldn't look for the worst in every gesture, is that what you're telling me?'

'Give the man a cigar,' she teased.

'I can see I'm going to have my hands full with you,' he said with a laugh. 'When did you get your degree in psychology?'

'It came with my journalism degree. We were taught to look for the motives in people's actions, the reasons why they behave as they do.'

He stood up and swung his leg over the chair, then opened his arms to her. 'I know how I plan to behave for the next few minutes, and my only motive is pure lust.'

Her eyes sparkled as she moved into the circle of his arms and moulded herself to him. His thrusting response sparked a matching desire within her, and she hooked her arms around his neck. 'It doesn't take a degree in psychology to work that out,' she assured him.

Making love in the afternoon played havoc with one's work schedule, she discovered. Only by applying herself to the typewriter with fierce concentration was she able to catch up on typing her notes. It was made even harder, because Rowan kept nuzzling the back of her neck as she typed.

'It's all right for you, you just send your film back to Sydney, and Tony does the hard work,' she complained.

'The hard work?' he queried dangerously.

'Some of it, anyway,' she said doggedly.

'I've a good mind to make you eat those words,' he threatened.

'If you distract me much more, that's all I'll be eating, because I'll miss my deadline and be out on my ear.'

'What a pity! Such beautiful ears, too.' He nibbled at the top of one to prove his point.

His warm breath danced over her cheek, and she sucked her own in tightly in response. 'This isn't getting the work done,' she repeated, her eyes on his face.

'I could take you away from all this,' he said, his tone teasing.

Her heart did a somersault. 'That almost sounds like a proposal.'

He shrugged. 'You never know your luck. In fact, it might be a good idea, now I've seen the way Laurie Bedford looks at you.'

She felt a pang of alarm. Hadn't he learned anything from their talk earlier? Now he was even talking about marrying her to stop another man from looking at her. It didn't bode well for their future if she couldn't make him see that with love came trust. She was still learning the lesson herself, but it had to work both ways. 'Then, for Laurie's sake, it's just as well we're both joking,' she said with forced lightness.

Despite her resolve, his teasing words haunted her as she tried to organise her thoughts on paper. She was sorely tempted to throw caution to the wind and agree to marry Rowan, for she was sure his proposal wasn't entirely tongue-in-cheek. But something stilled her voice. She knew it wouldn't be wise to say yes until he asked her for the right reasons.

Keeping her away from Laurie Bedford wasn't one of those reasons.

All the same, it was hard to keep her mind on her work, even though Rowan left her alone once he realised she was serious about finishing her article. Once or twice, he looked over her shoulder and made encouraging comments.

At last she pulled the final sheet out of the typewriter and sat back with a yelp of triumph. She passed the stack of notes to Rowan. 'What do you think?'

He read in silence for a while then put the notes beside her typewriter and leaned across to kiss her. 'A first-rate job, I'd say. Vera Philmont doesn't know what she lost when you left.'

Her mouth was still warm from the touch of his lips and she smiled, as much at the lingering taste of him as at the compliment. 'Thanks. I hope my editor agrees with you.' She pushed damp strands of hair back from her forehead. 'Whoever said journalism was exotic and fun? I'm worn out.'

His answering smile was wolfish. 'Maybe you should go to bed for a while.'

She grinned. 'I said I needed to rest.'

He affected an air of wide-eyed innocence. 'I believe that's what I just suggested.'

He ducked as she aimed a cushion at him, and it sailed harmlessly past. 'Witch!' he snarled. 'I've a good mind to teach you a few manners, but since you're tired, I'll let you off this once. Seriously, though, why don't you take some time off? You've been working flat out since you started this assignment.'

'Well, Ray does need the articles in a hurry. I can get the ones I've finished off to him tomorrow from Cessnock. He won't need the rest for a few days, so I could take some time off then.'

Rowan stood up and stretched. 'Then it's settled. We'll go into Cessnock tomorrow, get your articles on their way by courier, then paint the town red.'

'It's a large centre, but still fairly conservative,' she reminded him. 'Better make that dark pink.'

He nodded. 'You've got yourself a date, lady.'

There was a new warmth between them as they drove to Cessnock next morning. Although she gave her attention to the scenery, Danni's eyes kept straying to Rowan, as she thought how much he had come to mean to her.

What a pair they made—he so distrustful of women, thanks to his mother, and she equally suspicious of any man who had once owed allegiance to Trina. She almost laughed aloud as she thought of all that had passed between them since they came to the Hunter Valley. Once bitten—or more than once, in her case—had not made either of them as shy as they had believed when they first met.

At her suppressed giggle, his eyes swung from the road to her. 'What's so amusing?'

'Us,' she responded. 'I was just thinking what an unlikely couple we make.'

He chose to take her remark seriously. 'I don't know. We're both creative types who know what they want from life. And we're both sexy as hell.'

'He says modestly,' she added.

'You mean I'm not?'

If he hadn't been driving, she'd have thrown something at him. 'You know the answer to that. Although I'll admit it was a novel discovery for myself.'

Abruptly, he became serious. 'I know, Danni. I didn't have the wrong idea about you for a minute.'

Although they hadn't discussed it, he had known instinctively that she wasn't given to casual affairs. In fact, discovering the depths and intensity of her own sexual drives had come as a revelation. Even thinking about Rowan's lovemaking made her pulses quicken, and engendered a throbbing vivacity which pulsated through her entire body. She had never felt so alive as when she was with this man, in or out of his bed. He was like a firelighter to the kindling of her being. It was disquieting to think she already needed him so much.

They drove on in thoughtful silence. Gradually the vineyards, orchards and pastures gave way to the outskirts and then the centre of Cessnock, the industrial heart of the Hunter Valley. It was not a scenic city, being dominated by the potteries, pipeworks, brickyards, sawmills and factories which supported the surrounding countryside.

But it did have its own character, exuding an air of vitality and progress. From somewhere, Danni's journalistic mind dredged up the origins of its name. The original Scottish settler had named his grazing run Cessnock, most probably after a poem by his countryman, Robert Burns.

How homesick that pioneer must have been, to name his new land to remind him of his old country! Never mind that a glen was a mountain valley. The settlers still felt impelled to baptise the strange flat acres of wheat farm, vineyard and sheep run with the traditional names.

Reaching the centre of town, Rowan swung Danni's car into a vacant parking space near the main intersection. They had tossed a coin to see whose car they drove. Danni was glad she had won, because they had also agreed to share the driving. Handling Rowan's powerful sports car was something she would prefer to save for another time, preferably when she was on familiar roads.

Rowan cut the engine and handed her the keys, then uncoiled his legs from around the steering column. Watching him, Danni felt a brief pang of guilt. Maybe he would have been more comfortable in his own car. But he assured her he felt fine and they set off for the post office so that Danni could send the first of her copy by courier to Ray Conreid.

At the same time, they sent off the first batch of Rowan's film, so that it could be processed while Rowan was finishing the assignment. 'You're not sorry you didn't go to Hawaii?' Danni asked while they were waiting to be attended to.

He gave her a caressing look which sent shivers of desire down her spine, and she gripped the polished countertop as if her knees would buckle at any moment. 'Right now, there's nowhere on earth I would rather be than right here,' he murmured for her ears alone.

She walked out of the post office on winged feet, and looked around, seeing the centre through unashamedly rose-coloured glasses. 'What shall we do next?'

He hesitated, his hand warm on her arm. 'Cessnock has an excellent shopping centre. Would you like to look around while I hunt up some bits and pieces? My camera case snapped a buckle, and I'd like to replace it if I can.'

She looked at him in surprise, finding she was dismayed by the idea of them splitting up, even for a short time. 'I don't mind waiting while you do your errands.'

'I know, but I need a part for one of my cameras as well, and it may take me some time. You'd have more fun browsing through the shops.' There was a pretty little café facing them across the road, and he gestured towards it. 'We can meet up there and have lunch together. How's that?'

'All right, I suppose.'

'Fine. So let's meet back here at twelve-thirty, OK?'

'Very well, but...'

There were no buts. He was already striding off down the street, leaving her feeling a little bewildered. It was almost as if he had wanted to escape from her for a while.

Danni told herself she was being foolish. She had chided him for being overly possessive, and here she was, exhibiting the same trait! It would do them good to be apart for a short time. They had been together almost constantly since this assignment started.

Feeling better, she set off to explore the shopping centre. It offered a variety of small boutiques and larger stores. She scorned the latter, assuming they would stock much the same merchandise as their counterparts in Sydney, and spent a happy morning browsing among the smaller stores.

For her efforts, she found a hand-painted silk scarf by a local artist, which she was sure would delight Trina. At the last minute, she also bought a pair of gold cuff-links, fashioned into tiny bunches of grapes. This was for Rowan, and she clutched the small gift box happily, quickening her steps as she approached their agreed rendezvous. He would be surprised that she had bought him anything, since there was no special occasion. Except that every day was an occasion with him, she added to herself.

She was a few minutes late arriving outside the café, but all the kerbside tables were empty, so she was still ahead of Rowan. As a precaution, she glanced inside, but he was not among the diners there. She settled down at one of the outdoor tables, under a gaily striped umbrella, and ordered a cool drink for herself while she waited.

At first she was content to sip her drink and watch the passing parade. Then, as time passed, she began to feel the first prickles of concern. Rowan was so critical on unpunctuality in other people that it seemed unlikely he would be late himself.

When three-quarters of an hour passed with no sign of him, she decided to go looking. But her visits to the largest camera stores in the centre were in vain. None of the sales people remembered Rowan calling in. Twice, she returned to the café to see if he had arrived, but to no avail. What was she going to do?

On an impulse, she rang Bedales and asked whether Mr Traynor had returned there for some reason. But he hadn't, and Laurie Bedford was also out for the day, so there was no one to whom she could turn.

Common sense told her that he had met someone, or got tied up on some business matter. Maybe she should just go back to Bedales and wait for him there. At least she would be reachable by telephone if he was stranded in Cessnock. Here, he had no means of getting in touch with her. Neither had the police, nor anyone else, she thought, feeling a chill wash over her. If anything had happened to Rowan, they would try to reach her at the winery before looking anywhere else.

The drive back seemed endless, and she was exhausted by the time she arrived back at her cabin. There was still no word from Rowan, nor any sign of Laurie. She had never felt so alone or so helpless.

Her mood swung between anger at Rowan for leaving her high and dry like this, to terror that he had met with some accident. Finally, she could stand the suspense no longer, and decided to drive back the way she had come. She could also make enquiries at the police station, and at the hospital. Both would be quicker by telephone, she knew, but told herself she wasn't afraid to hear the worst. It was just that she would be on hand if Rowan needed her and she went in person.

'If Mr Traynor should call, tell him . . . tell him . . . oh, tell him to wait here until I get back,' she told the receptionist before she left Bedales.

This was getting monotonous, she told herself grimly as she set off along the Cessnock road for the third time that day. She would kill Rowan if there was a frivolous reason behind his disappearance.

A petrol station loomed in the distance, and reflexively she checked her fuel supply. If she ran out of petrol here, there would be two people on the missing list. As her gaze swept over the activities at the service station, she was suddenly riveted by the sight of a familiar car. Surely that silver station wagon belonged to Laurie?

Tears of relief that she had found someone to help her at last froze on her cheeks as she recognised another figure beside the station wagon.

The bonnet was up, and bending into the engine was Rowan himself. As she watched, perplexed, the passenger door opened and Trina stepped out.

Danni felt as if she was watching a silent movie, so detached and cold did she feel suddenly. As Trina came up behind him, Rowan straightened and wiped his hands on an oily rag. He said something to Trina and she laughed in response, sending a chill down Danni's spine. Then he leaned forward and carefully wiped a smudge of oil off Trina's cheek.

Automatically, Danni looked around for Laurie, but could see no sign of the winemaker. The car was empty, and there was no one else in front of the service station. This didn't make sense.

But even as she told herself she would do the grown-up thing and approach Rowan so he could explain what was going on, her right foot acted of its own accord and slammed the accelerator flat to the floor. Hauling her car around in a screech of protesting rubber, she headed back towards Bedales.

CHAPTER TEN

'STUPID, stupid, stupid!'

Danni muttered aloud as she poured a glass of wine for herself, then left it sitting on the countertop as she prowled around the cabin. Driving away had been a childish impulse. She should have stopped and asked Rowan what was going on. Whatever the explanation was, it couldn't be worse than the self-torture she was enduring now.

She reached for her wine glass and sat down, forcing herself to take a few cooling sips as she tried to marshal her thoughts. She was a journalist, accustomed to cool, analytical thinking. Why couldn't she apply some of it to this situation?

What exactly had she seen? Rowan and her sister, apparently suffering some sort of car trouble on the drive back to Bedales. It could mean that Trina had run into Rowan in Cessnock and offered him a lift back. But why hadn't he told Danni, instead of leaving her to wait and worry when he didn't show up? And what was Trina doing here, and in Laurie Bedford's car?

Trina could have turned the tables and convinced Rowan she was Danni. No, Danni dismissed this thought out of hand. When they switched places before, Rowan hadn't been fooled. Besides, why would Trina want to do such a thing?

After a while, Danni's head began to ache with the strain of trying to work it all out. She was already tired after working too hard for the last few days, with the added stress of worrying about Rowan's whereabouts. She was in no shape to think rationally about anything.

Deliberately, she took a steadying breath. Rowan and Trina were obviously on their way to Bedales. She resolved to wait and see what they had to say when they got here or sent a message.

A message! Why hadn't she thought of it before? Rowan could have left a message with the winery receptionist, but Danni had been too distressed by her own fantasies to think of checking with her. Resolutely, she picked up the telephone.

Before she could dial the front desk, however, there was the sound of a car pulling up outside. Her breath caught in her throat and her heart turned a painful somersault as fear gripped her. But what was she so frightened of? She didn't know which scared her the most—the thought of losing Rowan, or the possibility that she had already done so.

'That's enough,' she told herself firmly. There was no point in tormenting herself with such thoughts when she had only to wait a few more minutes to know the truth.

Nevertheless, she had trouble controlling the tremors which engulfed her as she went to open the cabin door. Outside, Laurie was helping Trina out of the car, while Rowan lifted some luggage out of the back seat.

It took her a moment to absorb the fact that Laurie was part of the group. Had he been with them all along? Before she could say anything, Laurie gave them a cheery wave and headed across the grass to the main building saying, 'Thanks for your help, Rowan. Don't forget that new wine I promised to let you taste.'

Rowan looked up and caught sight of her framed in the cabin doorway. One look at her distressed expression must have told him how she was feeling. He came over to her. 'There's no need to look so terrified. As I told you in my message, it was only a breakdown. I'm sorry as hell about the mix-up earlier, but...'

'Then you *did* leave a message,' she interrupted in a whisper.

'With the receptionist, but you'd already left again. Didn't you check with her when you got back?'

Danni shook her head. 'I was too anxious to think of checking with her.'

'My God, you must be nearly out of your mind!'

She nodded, dangerously close to breaking down in tears. 'I didn't know what to think.'

He took her arm, his grip warm and strong, the strength of it flowing into her like a current. 'Let's go inside and talk.' He glanced over his shoulder at Trina, waiting beside the car. 'Can you give us a few minutes?'

'Sure, take your time. I'll get the rest of my things out of the car.'

Inside the cabin, Rowan guided her to a chair and pushed her gently into it. 'You thought I'd gone off with Trina, didn't you?'

'No, of course not!'

'Then why do you look as if your world has come to an end?'

She had no defence against this, because he was right. 'All right, I was thinking the worst,' she confessed.

His mouth twisted into a wry grin. 'In that case, we're about even.'

Her eyebrows lifted. 'What do you mean?'

'Earlier today, I thought you were the one two-timing me, when I saw you going off with Laurie Bedford just before we were due to meet for lunch.'

'Going off with Laurie? But I haven't seen him all day.'

'I know that now. It was Trina I saw getting into his car, but from a distance I thought it was you. God, you've no idea how murderous I felt.'

Her spirits had begun to lift, and now they soared. 'Yes, I do. I've been feeling exactly the same way.' Shamefacedly, but determined to make a clean breast of her actions, she explained about driving back towards Cessnock to look for him. 'When I saw you and Trina together, with no sign of Laurie, I went a little crazy. I just put my foot down and drove flat out back here without even stopping to think.'

He tilted her chin in his hand, so their eyes met. His gaze seared her with its burning intensity. 'I think we're both a little crazy when it comes to each other. Even our past problems aren't enough to explain it. I thought it was fear that you'd leave me the way my mother left my father, but it's even simpler than that. You're the best thing that's ever happened to me, Danni, and I'm terrified of losing you.'

She stood up and went into his arms, the strength of his embrace telling her how he felt more surely than any words. She returned the pressure, running her hands up and down his back, as if playing a cherished instrument. The tune she heard was the singing of her heart, released from its fears.

His mouth plundered hers with hungry eagerness, and she opened her lips to his with answering passion. They kissed until the quivering tension in their bodies cried out for release; then they both remembered their responsibilities at the same time.

'Trina, she's still outside,' Danni said when she had control of her breathing again.

'Damn Trina and the whole world!' he said savagely. 'All I can think of right now is how much I love you.'

Carefully, she moved out of the circle of his arms and poured a glass of wine, handing it to him. 'There'll be plenty of other times just for us,' she assured him in a passion-drugged voice. 'We can wait.'

'Speak for yourself,' he growled back, but laughed as control began to return and his breathing steadied. 'But you're right, I suppose. As long as the waiting isn't too long.'

'It won't be,' she promised. After the waiting she had done today, a little longer hardly mattered, but she knew that Rowan was less patient. 'Tell me,' she said to distract them both, 'what exactly happened in Cessnock this morning?'

He took a swallow of his drink, then set it down. 'I was on my way to meet you as we'd agreed, then I saw what I thought was you going off with Laurie to his car. When I caught up with them, I found out that Trina had come up here looking for a shoulder to cry on, and run into Laurie. He also mistook Trina for you, and had stopped to see if you wanted a lift, when he found himself talking to your twin. Once they had introduced themselves, he volunteered to drive her out here. By the time I'd caught up with them and sorted everything out, you'd left the café and I didn't know where to look for you. I knew you had the car keys with you, so I hoped you would head back here eventually. I asked Laurie and Trina to drive me back, but we had a breakdown on the way. When you saw us, I was puzzling over the engine and Laurie was inside the garage, talking to the mechanic.'

She let out an exasperated breath. 'What a mix-up! I kept telling myself there was a logical explanation for what had happened, but I couldn't think what it was.'

'Except that I had to be lying about my relationship with your sister,' he finished for her. When she looked away, he turned her head back to him and kissed her lightly on the lips. 'It's all right, I understand how you arrived at your conclusions. That's why I want to make sure nothing like this can ever happen again.'

'How are you going to do that?'

He reached into his pocket and drew out a dark blue velvet jeweller's case. Opening it, he offered it to her. 'By giving you this.'

Involuntarily, she caught her breath. Nestling in the box was a marquise-cut solitaire diamond set on a slender, white-gold band. 'You bought this for me today?'

'That's right. Why do you think I was so anxious to get away from you for a while? I wanted to present this to you at lunch, never dreaming how things would turn out. Will you accept it now and agree to marry me?'

Of all the reasons why he might have wanted to be alone, she had never guessed the right one. She turned shining eyes to him. 'Yes, Rowan. With all my heart.'

Letting his breath out in a hissing sigh which revealed the depth of his uncertainty, he lifted the ring out of its box and slipped it on to the third finger of her left hand. 'Damn, it's a little loose. I was sure I'd got the size right.'

She traced a finger down the side of his face, skipping across the trace of new beard, and ending at his mouth, where he kissed the teasing finger. 'Don't worry, it's the most beautiful ring in the world,' she assured him. If it had been a cigar wrapper, she couldn't have been happier than she was at this moment!

'All the same, we'll have it adjusted when we're back in Sydney. I want everything to be perfect for you.'

She looked up at him with wide-eyed delight. 'It already is perfect.'

Suddenly, their eyes locked as they remembered at the same moment. 'Trina!'

She had also tired of waiting outside, because
she chose that moment to peer around the cabin
door. 'Can I come inside now?'

'Of course,' Danni said, her voice vibrant with
happiness. Then she remembered that Trina had
problems of her own. Now might not be the most
tactful moment to break the news of Rowan's proposal and her acceptance. She shot a warning glance
at Rowan, and he nodded slightly.

'You two must have a lot to talk about,' he said
awkwardly. 'I'll be over at the tasting-room with
Laurie if you need me.'

She would always need him, Danni's look plainly
told him, but she appreciated his tact. She was
anxious to find out what had brought Trina up here
unannounced. It had to be something to do with
her volatile romance with the American called
Malcolm. She waited until Rowan had gone, then
curled up on the couch opposite her twin. 'This is
a surprise,' she began.

'So Rowan said.' Trina giggled. 'When he saw
me at the bus station in Cessnock, he thought I was
you. For a minute, I was tempted to let him think
so. He's quite a man, isn't he?'

Danni felt the first stirrings of anxiety. Surely
Trina hadn't come up here with the idea of re-
kindling an affair with Rowan? 'I think he is,' she
said carefully. 'He tells me things aren't the best
between you and Malcolm.'

Trina pulled a face. 'Malcolm was a mistake from
the beginning. I found that out when I went with
him to meet his family in Surfers' Paradise.'

'Didn't you get along with them?' Danni asked.

'I was fine. I get along well with everybody. *They* were the problem. They're what's called "old money" in the United States. His mother made it clear that I wasn't in their class—Irish descent, probably convict ancestors.'

'What did she say?'

Trina shrugged. 'It wasn't what she said, as much as the way she said it. She thought having a father who wrote poetry was quaint, and told me that she had a very charming maid called Trina. Oh, it was all very civilised, but she made it clear that I wasn't good enough for her Malcolm.'

'But if you love him...'

'Love him?' Trina cut in. 'He didn't say a word to defend me! Just sat back while his parents ran me into the floor and then ground me underneath their Gucci heels! I packed up and caught the first plane back to Sydney. Rowan was nice to me, but then he hared off up here and I was left with nobody.'

Out of the heights of her new-found happiness, Danni felt more compassion for her sister than ever before. 'It was a rotten deal,' she agreed. 'But there'll be other men. If Malcolm wasn't man enough to stand up for you, you're better off without him anyway.'

'It's easy enough for you to say,' Trina spat out with a venom which caught Danni by surprise. 'You've always got what you wanted, so you don't know what it's like to be left behind.'

In consternation, Danni stared at her twin. 'Left behind? You've never been left behind in anything.

You wouldn't even say such a thing if you weren't so upset.'

'I know what I'm saying,' Trina averred. 'And it's the truth. Everything's always been easy for you because you're the one with the brains. Everybody knew you would succeed at whatever you set out to do.'

'Only because I couldn't compete with you in looks,' Danni breathed. 'You were always so beautiful. Even though we had the same features, you had something extra which made people's heads turn.'

'I didn't have much choice, did I? Looks were all I had left, since you took the top spot in every class we were in. I couldn't compete with that, and I hated studying, while you seemed to thrive on it. I set out to make the best of my looks so I could outshine you at something, at least.'

Danni had never suspected that her twin envied her academic success. 'I always envied *you*,' she said in a startled tone. 'You seemed to get dates so easily, while I had to practically ask someone to take me to the school dances.'

'Only because they were in awe of you,' Trina told her sharply. 'They were scared they couldn't keep up with you. They told me so.'

'I never knew. I thought it was because they preferred your sense of fun.'

'Fun, hah!' Trina almost spat out. 'It was the biggest act of my life, pretending to be the good-time girl. There were times when I wanted to kill you for being so smart.'

Shock made Danni clench the arms of her chair until her knuckles whitened. 'Trina, don't say that! You don't mean it.'

'Yes, I do,' her twin insisted. 'Our parents were always so proud of you. They knew they'd never have to worry about your future, but they used to speculate about finding a good husband for me, so I'd be looked after.' Her voice broke on a sob. '*Looked after*—as if I was a half-wit.'

'I'm sure they didn't think any such thing. They were only concerned about you, because you seemed to think about nothing except having a good time.' Desperately, she searched for something to reassure her twin that she was wrong, then she had it. 'What about Keith Bowden? I was going to marry him, until I found out he was only seeing me so he could be close to you.'

But to her surprise, Trina reacted with disgust. 'That brainless hunk? You were better off without him. He only wanted one thing, and he knew he wouldn't get it from you without putting a ring on your finger. He thought he'd have a better chance with me.' She laughed bitterly. 'I found out from Keith that I had what we used to call a reputation. Isn't that something?'

Feeling as if Trina had struck her a physical blow, Danni reeled back in her chair. All these years she had blamed Trina for taking Keith away from her, she'd been stupidly mistaken. Keith had left her, not because he preferred her twin, but because he knew she would never sleep with him until they were committed to each other. All along, Keith had only wanted sex, while letting her think he cared. How he must have laughed when he saw how despondent she had been when he left her!

She felt as if someone was shaking the very foundations of her being. For so long, she had thought Trina was the blessed one, breezing through life without a care. When all along her twin had envied *her!* It was almost too much to take in. She shook her head tiredly. 'I don't understand any of this, Trina. Why didn't you ever tell me how you felt?'

'Having you pity me would have been the final humiliation. You'd have liked that, wouldn't you?'

'No, I'd have tried to help.' She could see from Trina's expression that she was wasting her words. Her twin had existed for so long on her jealousy of Danni that nothing she could say would change anything. She decided to try another approach. 'You're a success in your career,' she observed. 'Doesn't that mean anything to you?'

'What else could I be but a model?' Trina asked bitterly. 'And even in modelling, looks like mine are as common as sand on the beach.'

'Was that why you did the centrefold—to try to make a name for yourself?'

Violently, Trina shook her head. Then she said, in a voice barely above a whisper, 'I did it because it was the one thing I knew you would never do.'

'You put your body on display to the world to spite me? I can't believe you'd go that far.'

'Believe it,' Trina stated. 'It worked, didn't it? Everybody thought it was you, and you got thrown out of your job because of it.'

'You sound as if you're pleased.'

'As a matter of fact, I was. For the first time, we were even, and not even your fancy IQ could get you out of that one. But even then, you had the last laugh. Who ever thought that Rowan would fall for you?'

'Why should it matter to you?' Danni asked tautly. 'There was nothing between you two, Rowan told me so. You were already dating Malcolm.'

'That was a slight oversight,' Trina said unpleasantly. 'And one I came up here to rectify.'

Danni's breath caught in her throat as she listened to Trina's matter-of-fact tone. For a crazy moment, she felt vulnerable, as if Trina could make good her vow. Then she felt the cool ring of gold around her finger, and some of Rowan's strength flowed into her from it. 'I'm afraid it's too late,' she told Trina quietly. 'You see, this afternoon Rowan asked me to marry him, and I accepted.'

Anger blazed in her twin's eyes. 'I don't believe you!'

Silently, Danni held out her left hand, and the diamond winked mockingly up at Trina.

For a moment, she stared at the ring, transfixed. Then blazing fury erupted on her face. Danni had never seen her twin so possessed. 'I should have known!' she seethed. 'You always have to come out the winner, don't you? Even in love.'

'Trina, don't,' Danni begged, hating and fearing the blackness of her sister's expression. 'We can work this out.'

'How?' challenged Trina. 'By letting me be your pretty little bridesmaid?'

Before Danni could stop her, she jumped up, wrenched open the cabin door and ran blindly out into the vineyard.

Numbed by pain and shock, Danni remained where she was, trying to make sense of the last few minutes. All the time they were growing up together, she had never dreamed that Trina felt this way. If she had only said something, they might have talked it out. Instead, she had bottled everything up, finally turning her frustrations against herself by posing nude for a men's magazine.

Desperately, Danni wished that her parents still lived in Australia. More than anything, she needed their wise counsel and guidance as to how she should handle the situation.

Trina needed help, that was obvious, but Danni—for all the brains Trina so envied—hadn't a clue what to do.

As she sat with her hands clenched in her lap, her back ramrod straight, she became aware of a distant noise, like thunder approaching. It nagged at the rim of her consciousness, familiar and somehow dangerous, but she was too preoccupied to work it out.

Suddenly she had it, and in the same second, she leapt to her feet, her heart in her mouth.

She reached the back of the cabins in time to see her worst fears realised. The tractor pulling the grass-clearing mechanism was working near the cabins. It was the same one she had so nearly walked under, until Laurie had pulled her clear. The same driver was working it, his head swathed in the protective ear-muffs.

Walking towards the monster, her head down and her shoulders heaving, was Trina. She was too deeply immersed in her grief to be aware of the danger bearing down upon her.

'Trina, look out!' Danni screamed at the top of her lungs, but her voice was drowned out by the tractor's roar.

Blinded by tears, her sister didn't even look up.

With sickening clarity, Danni saw the whirling blades of the grass-cutter churning behind the tractor. They were seconds away from Trina's path.

All thoughts of the past few minutes fled from Danni's mind as she registered only one thing. Her twin was in terrible danger. Almost without conscious thought, she began to run, terror lending her feet wings.

As she ran, she prayed as she had never done before.

CHAPTER ELEVEN

JUST when Danni had given up hope, Trina looked up and screamed as she saw the monstrous blades whirling down upon her. She seemed to freeze in the path of the machine, like a rabbit transfixed by a shooter's spotlight.

The hope, which had flared briefly for Danni, died as she saw her twin freeze. The sun was in the driver's eyes. There was no way he would see Trina in time to avoid running over her.

Time seemed to stand still as Danni raced across the paddock. Her lungs were bursting and her throat was raw from her screams and the need to reach Trina.

Behind her, she was distantly aware of men shouting, but the tractor driver, high in his cabin, his ears swathed by headphones and his eyes blinded by sun, gave no sign that he noticed anything amiss.

Danni's worst nightmares had never felt as terrifying as this.

'Oh, God, Trina!' she sobbed, as she made a last mighty lunge for her twin. A series of sharp reports battered at her eardrums, and she had a fleeting glimpse of Rowan pointing a scatter-gun skywards and firing it repeatedly.

As if in slow motion, Danni saw the tractor driver's startled reaction as he heard the gun go off. Then he saw the two women almost underneath his wheels and hauled the tractor around in a desperate attempt to avoid them. In the same moment, Danni reached Trina and, with all her strength, thrust her sister out of the cutter's path.

Then the machine was upon them, and Danni felt a sickening blow strike her as one of the machine's outriders caught her from behind. She felt herself flying through the air, and had a horrifying vision of Trina lying sprawled amid the grapevines, before she landed in a crumpled heap herself and blackness rushed in to claim her.

There were voices, lots of voices, all talking at once. Hands explored her limp body, and someone tried to pick her up. She was about to cry out in protest when other, stronger arms closed around her, and she knew instinctively that she was safe. She was tired, so dreadfully tired. It was heaven to rest her aching head against the hardness of a masculine chest and allow herself to be spirited to somewhere warm and comfortable, where she could sleep as she longed to do.

She knew a terrible moment of loss when she was placed upon a yielding surface and covered gently. The arms which had sustained and comforted her were gone. Where? She felt alone and bereft.

Above her, lights slid by in a sparkling stream, and there were more voices. Then something cold and sharp slid into her arm and she knew nothing more.

She awoke to find herself in a hard, high bed with a screen placed to one side so she couldn't see beyond it. A hand caressed her forehead, and she looked up into Rowan's cobalt eyes. 'Have I been asleep long?'

'The usual question is "where am I?"' he observed, cradling her fingers in his hand. 'I might have known you'd be more original. You've been out for an hour, no more. And to answer your unspoken question, you're in hospital in Cessnock.'

'Hospital?' Suddenly, the events of the last few hours came hurtling into her mind, and she gripped his hand convulsively. 'Trina? Is she all right?'

A shadow crossed his face. 'She's asleep. But you saved her life, getting her out of the path of that cutter.'

Decisively, she shook her head, then closed her eyes against the wave of pain the movement caused. 'No, it was you. You fired the scatter-gun and alerted the driver.'

'But he couldn't react in time, and I wasn't close enough to get to Trina. If you hadn't pushed her out of the way...' He tailed off.

'Is she really all right?'

'She will be. She landed pretty heavily and hit her head on a rock. The tractor just caught you a glancing blow from behind. Apart from a few bruises and shock, the doctor tells me you'll be fine.'

Something in his voice alerted her. 'What do you mean, Trina will be all right?'

He took a deep breath, and his hand closed around her more tightly. 'All right, she's in a coma.'

Her eyes widened with horror. 'A coma? Isn't that serious?'

'It depends. The way the doctor explained it to me, there are different kinds and degrees. In Trina's case, it was probably caused by the trauma of hitting her head, but she is responding to some stimuli, so they don't think it will take her long to come out of it.'

'But she *will* come out of it?' Her voice vibrated with fear.

'The doctors think so. We just have to be patient.'

Danni turned her head away, so he wouldn't see the tears which were dangerously close to the surface. It was all very well for Rowan to counsel patience, but he didn't know why Trina had been running across the field in the first place. 'It's all my fault that she's like this,' she said miserably.

'Don't be ridiculous. I just told you that you saved her life.'

'I wouldn't have needed to, if I'd been more sensitive in the first place.'

He perched himself on the side of her bed so she had no option but to look at him. 'Now, tell me the reason for this orgy of self-recrimination,' he said.

Haltingly, she told him about the awful scene in the cabin after he left them alone. 'She came here to try to patch things up with you, and I told her we were engaged. I should have waited. If only I'd found a gentler way to break it to her, this wouldn't have happened.'

'You don't know that.' He looked up hopefully as the screen was pushed aside and a nurse came into the cubicle. 'Has Trina Dare come around yet?' he asked for them both.

Her fingers resting on Danni's wrist, the nurse shook her head. 'I'm afraid not. I just heard the doctor talking, and he said it's the darnedest thing. She didn't sustain enough damage to drive her into a coma. It's as if she doesn't want to wake up.'

'It's as if she doesn't want to wake up.' The words haunted Danni throughout the following day and night, when there was still no change in Trina's condition. How could Rowan say she wasn't to blame, when the nurse put it as plainly as that?

So she could be near Trina, she accepted Laurie's offer to recuperate at Bedales. Although her injuries had soon healed, her doctor recommended as much rest as possible to ensure a complete recovery before she went back to her normal life.

But how could anything be normal when she and Laurie went every day to visit her sister who lay in her hospital bed, her life sustained by tubes running into and out of her body?

'She looks as if she's merely sleeping,' she whispered to Laurie as they stood by Trina's bedside on one such visit.

'It *is* a kind of sleep,' he confirmed. 'But it's got the doctors puzzled. When they tested her, she responded to a whole range of stimuli, so they're convinced she could wake up if she wanted to.'

'You make it sound so simple.'

'Maybe it is. If we just knew why she doesn't want to face the world, maybe we could get through to her. She's supposed to be able to hear us talking, even though she can't or won't respond.'

Danni knew why Trina didn't want to face the world. Now that she knew about Rowan and Danni, she had nothing left to live for. First Malcolm had deserted her, and now Rowan. It was more than she could handle.

There was no hope that Trina and Malcolm would reconcile their differences. In a Sunday gossip column, Danni had read that the business tycoon had returned to America to take over his family business. Old money, no doubt, Danni thought sourly. Poor Trina.

There was nothing to do except sit with Trina for as long as possible. Danni's injuries had healed and, away from the hospital, she prowled around her cabin like a ghost. She tried to work, but the words came out trite and meaningless. Savagely, she tore another sheet of typing out of her machine, crumpled it into a ball and hurled it across the cabin to join the growing pile.

What was happening to her? Since the accident, she had been unable to concentrate on anything. Maybe she should go back to the hospital for another check-up.

It wouldn't help, she knew. What ailed her wasn't physical. She was hopelessly in love with Rowan, but the certainty was growing that she couldn't marry him now.

Laurie had invited her to stay here and write the history of Bedales. Hoping to persuade her, he had brought her a stack of reference books about the area, but she couldn't concentrate enough to read any of them right through. Committing herself to the project meant letting Rowan go back to Sydney without her. She had never felt so confused before.

How could she make a decision when she didn't
know what was right any more?

She was sitting on a bench outside her cabin, surrounded by Laurie's reference books, when Rowan
came up to her. 'Are you sure you're up to working
already?'

'No, but I have to do something or I'll go crazy.'

He looked at the book titles. 'These aren't for
the investment series, surely?'

'No. I'm thinking of writing the history of
Bedales.'

His searching gaze made her look away. 'You
would need to spend a long time up here for a
project of that size,' he observed.

She kept her voice steady with an effort. 'Yes, I
would.'

'Are you forgetting that you agreed to marry
me?' he asked, his voice taut. 'While you recovered, I kept my distance, but if you're well
enough to make plans, don't you think they should
include me?'

The pain in his voice drew her eyes upwards until
they locked with his. She was shocked by the despair she saw there. But it was no more than a reflection of her own inner turmoil. Somehow she
had to make him understand how she felt. 'I can't
marry you now, not the way things are,' she tried.

'How are they?' he demanded. 'Come on, tell
me. Just how are they? Have you discovered you
love Bedford, after all? You've been spending
enough time with him lately, and now you're doing
his book.'

'No! He comes to the hospital because he wants to see Trina, that's all.'

'Then if it isn't him, what is it?'

'Can't you see? Our love almost got my sister killed. How can I be happy when I know what I've done to her?'

His face contorted with anger and suffering. 'Denying yourself won't change anything.'

'I know, but what else can I do? I love you, Rowan, more than life itself. You must know it by now.'

'How can I when you're prepared to sacrifice our future to assuage your guilt? Trina walked under the tractor, for pity's sake. You didn't push her.'

'I might as well have,' she said bitterly. 'She came to me because she was hurting. If I hadn't blurted out that we were engaged, she wouldn't have rushed out and been injured.'

'So you're going to do penance for the rest of your life?'

'I don't know what I'm going to do. Oh, God, Rowan! What if she never wakes up?'

'Don't, Danni. You're tearing me apart. I love you, and I want you to be my wife. Nothing else can be allowed to matter.'

She shook her head. 'It's not that simple. If I marry you, I'll always remember what my happiness cost my sister.' Her eyes blurred with tears as she fought to make him understand.

He looked dazed as he fumbled in his pocket. 'Then you won't take this back?'

He held out the diamond ring he had placed on her finger just before the accident. In her desperation to reach Trina, it had flown from her hand and been lost. She had looked for it in the paddock when she came back, but had assumed it was lost beyond recovery. 'I can't,' she said miserably.

'I went to some trouble to make sure it would fit this time,' he said in a detached voice. 'But it was never destined to fit, was it?'

'Don't say that. You *are* my destiny!' she cried, her heart going out to him. In a moment, he would be gone and her heart with him. Temptation warred inside her. The ring and all it meant lay in his hands. But she couldn't bring herself to reach for it, knowing what it had cost. 'God, Rowan, I'm so sorry,' she said, gulping air to stop herself from bursting into uncontrollable sobs.

'So am I,' he replied tonelessly. He looked at the ring, then dropped it into his pocket as if he never wanted to look at it again. 'So am I.'

He turned and the moment was upon them. Suddenly, she couldn't let him walk out of her life without leaving her with something to ease the dark times ahead. She flung herself at him and buried her face in his shoulder.

His arms tightened around her, as if he would never let go. Feverishly, his lips sought her face, her throat and then her mouth.

Desperation made her return his kisses with a hunger which seared her to her soul. How she loved him! Passion flamed between them, and she felt a fleeting sense of hope that everything might be all right. Then the vision of Trina, lying beyond reach in her hospital bed, returned and she turned to stone in Rowan's arms.

He felt her change. 'You really mean it, don't you? You're staying here?'

Dumbly, she nodded, her throat too tight for speech.

He detached himself from her arms. 'Then it's the end for us. There's no more to say.'

And he walked away. Every nerve in her body urged her to call him back, but she kept silent. The price was just too high.

Through a rainforest curtain of tears, she saw him throw his suitcase into his car and drive off, while the dust of his departure fell around her like the fallout from Armageddon.

After Rowan had left, the winery felt deserted, even though there were any number of people coming and going as Bedales continued its unrelenting cycle in harmony with nature.

The driver of the tractor, shocked by the harm his negligence had caused, had left before Laurie could fire him. Danni hadn't seen the man again after the accident, but Laurie had told her what happened.

She should have felt some rancour towards the driver but she felt nothing, nor for anything else which went on around her. Rowan's departure had left a void inside her which nothing seemed to fill.

The only time she felt alive was when she sat with Trina, talking to her, playing tapes of her favourite music and talking to Laurie in her hearing.

The only name Danni couldn't bring herself to mention was Rowan's. Although he haunted her every waking thought and came to her in dreams, it hurt too much to speak of him to anyone. Laurie must have noticed her missing engagement ring by now, but he made no comment.

The only bright spot on her horizon was the imminent arrival of her parents. Danni had contacted Sean and Beth O'Dare after the accident. They had arranged to fly out at once. She longed to see them again, although she wished it could have been in happier circumstances.

She was sitting outside her cabin at Bedales, trying to concentrate on some background reading, when she was hailed by a familiar male voice.

'So this is what you get up to the minute you're out of my sight!'

Danni looked up in surprise. 'Ray! What are you doing here?'

'Is that any way for a journalist to greet her editor?' he asked with mock severity.

She laughed for the first time in days. 'I'm surprised you're still my editor. I must have missed the deadline by ages.'

He took a seat opposite her and leaned forward. 'Not to worry about a little thing like a deadline. After all, you A-grade journalists can pick and choose your assignments.'

'A-grade?' she said in astonishment. 'But I'm still a B-grade.'

'Not now your Hunter Valley articles have started appearing,' he told her. 'As a result of the ones which have already appeared, we've picked up a lot of new subscribers among wine enthusiasts and frustrated vignerons.'

'But the series isn't finished yet.'

'I know, and our readers are anxiously awaiting the rest, but not until you're fully recovered from your accident. Mrs Philmont wanted you to know that.'

She could hardly believe her ears. 'Did Mrs Philmont send you all the way up here just to tell me to get well soon?'

His lop-sided grin rewarded her. 'Hardly. But she did suggest I come up here and offer you another job—as editor of her *Leisure and Money* magazine.'

An A-grading and a full editorship! It was almost too much to take in. 'But won't she worry that a centrefold girl will give such a flashy magazine a bad name?' she asked wickedly.

'I was also to tell you she's sorry about the misunderstanding,' he confessed. 'If she'd known it was your twin sister, she would never have let such a valuable journalist go.'

Danni gaped at him. 'But she knew all along it wasn't me!' The sly old woman was saving face by pretending otherwise. Now she had seen the effect Danni could have on her readers, she was anxious to reinstate her at all costs, preferably before some rival publication snapped her up. She laughed delightedly. 'Am I allowed time to think the offer over?'

'Take all the time you want,' Ray said gravely. 'I'm rather enjoying watching her stew in her own juice for a change!'

'You're awful, Ray,' she said, but secretly she agreed with him. It would do the powerful publisher good to find out she couldn't treat people as if they were pawns in her private chess game.

Ray had another surprise for her. 'I understand that another story came out of this assignment as well, what you could call a human interest story.'

Baffled, she frowned at him. 'I don't know of any.'

'I believe you got yourself engaged to Rowan Traynor between assignments.'

Her eyes widened. 'How did you find out?'

'Remember I told you that Laurie Bedford is a friend of Vera Philmont's? He rang to tell her the good news and, of course, she passed it on to me. I think that's another reason for the job offer. She's terrified that you might succumb to the lure of home and babies.'

'Tell her she has nothing to worry about, then.'

He swore softly. 'Oh-oh! Have I said something out of turn?'

'Not deliberately,' she hastened to reassure him. 'We were a bit hasty, that's all.' She didn't want to tell him that the engagement was completely off. It would entail too many explanations she didn't feel up to giving. 'We decided to think things over for a little longer.'

He looked relieved. 'Then you aren't upset because I let Traynor come up here instead of Donna Healey?'

'I could hardly get engaged to Donna Healey,' she said with forced good humour. In truth, she was thinking how differently everything would have turned out if Ray hadn't gone along with the switch. She and Rowan would never have become engaged, and Trina wouldn't be lying in a coma now. But she could hardly blame Ray for the vagaries of fate, so she masked her unhappiness. 'You meant well.'

'I'm glad you understand. But Traynor can be very persuasive when he wants to.'

How well Danni knew that! 'Let's not talk about him for now,' she said firmly. 'How are things back at the magazine?'

They talked shop for a little longer, but Ray, sensing her discomfort, cut it short. 'I understand you're still getting over your accident, so I'll be on my way. Can I tell Mrs Philmont you'll be in touch?'

Since she would be in need of a job once she left here, she had little choice but to say, 'Yes, you can tell her. And thank her for the offer. It's very generous of her.'

His wry look said he knew who Mrs Philmont was helping with her offer. After she walked him to his car and waved him away, Danni found she was exhausted.

CHAPTER TWELVE

THE days melted into one another as Danni either passed the time at Bedales, making a half-hearted start on the history project, or sat with Trina.

Her eyes were on the motionless figure in the bed, but she was hardly aware of what she had seen until it happened again—the tiniest movement of her sister's hand. Had she imagined it, or had Trina really moved her hand in response to something Danni had said? She had developed the habit of speaking her thoughts aloud, and she had been doing so just now. But what had she said to breach the barriers of Trina's unconsciousness?

Then she knew.

Her voice vibrant with emotion, she repeated, 'I feel so lonely, with you like this and Rowan out of my life.'

There it was again, the tiniest fluttering of Trina's fingers. And Danni understood. It was the first time she had spoken of her feelings for Rowan. 'Oh, Trina,' she said with a rush of emotion, 'I told Rowan I can't marry him. Not if it means destroying you. I'm so sorry I broke the news to you in such a brutal way. But it's going to be all right. I . . . I sent him away.'

'No!'

The single word sounded as if it had been wrenched from her sister's throat. Danni stared at

Trina, hope welling up like a living thing inside her. 'What did you say?'

Trina's eyes flickered open, and she turned her head very slightly towards Danni. 'No, you love him.'

Dashing away her tears of joy, Danni plunged for the alarm which would alert the medical staff. They came at once, and Danni was reluctantly ushered from her sister's side while they went to work.

It was much later before she was allowed back into Trina's room. To her relief, most of the life-support equipment had been moved aside, and Trina was half sitting up in her bed, her eyes open and unmistakably alert.

Danni rushed to her side and grasped her twin's hands, which were much thinner than she liked to feel. 'Trina, you're awake! It's true, you're going to be all right.'

'It's like a dream,' Trina said softly, as if her throat was still troubling her. 'You were talking to me, but it's as if there was a wall between us that I couldn't break through to reach you.'

'It's all right, there's no wall now.'

Trina dropped her long lashes over her brimming eyes. 'Yes, there is. You must marry Rowan.'

Danni shook her head. 'Don't think about it now. You must get well first.'

'But I *have* to think about it. I'll never forgive myself if you give him up because of me.'

Fiddling with the bedclothes, Danni kept her eyes averted. 'What makes you think it's because of you?'

'It has to be, because of—of what I said before I ran out and almost under that machine.' She grasped Danni's hands urgently. 'I'm so sorry for the things I said. I was so upset about what Malcolm and his family had put me through, I wasn't thinking properly. I didn't mean any of it. You've been a wonderful sister to me, although I don't deserve you.'

'Don't, please,' Danni begged, embarrassed. 'I never dreamed you felt inadequate around me. I thought it was the other way around.'

'You?' Trina laughed. 'You never had a moment's doubt about anything.'

Danni very quickly set her straight on that score, and the two ended up falling into one another's arms, on the verge of tears. 'Rowan was never right for me,' Trina admitted much later. 'He knew it as well as I did, so it would have ended whether you were on the scene or not. Malcolm was much more my type.' She looked around, as if expecting to find him in the room. 'I dreamed he was at my bedside all the time I was asleep.'

'That was Laurie Bedford,' Danni said unwillingly. 'He hardly left your side.'

Trina looked thoughtful. 'Hmmm. I must remember to thank him for caring so much.' From the look of Trina's expression, her way of thanking Laurie would have him swooning at her feet, Danni thought with some amusement. Wouldn't it be wonderful if…she chased the thought away before it was fully formed. Trina had to make her own mistakes from now on. They both did.

'I'm told you saved my life,' Trina said shyly as Danni was getting ready to leave.

'I didn't stop to think,' Danni confessed.

'Then that makes us about even, doesn't it? I'll never be able to remind you about that boating accident again.'

'It's an ill wind!' laughed Danni as she took her leave.

But her smile faded as soon as she was clear of her sister's room. She was immeasurably relieved that Trina had come around and would make a complete recovery. Laurie would be thrilled when he came to see her, which would be as soon as he finished a business meeting in Cessnock, Danni recalled.

She even had her sister's blessing for her engagement to Rowan Traynor. Except that there was no engagement, and it wasn't likely that he would ask her again.

Stupidly, she had driven him out of her life, thinking she couldn't take her happiness at the expense of Trina's, when Trina—supposedly less wise—had pointed out how foolish that was.

Blind to the hustle and bustle of the hospital corridor, she leaned weakly against a wall. Suddenly the prospect of a new job and greater career success seemed to pale. How could she look forward to a future which didn't include the man she loved?

Her heart began to race, until she wondered if she was having some sort of attack. Then she realised it was thoughts of Rowan which made her pulses race so, and her body temperature start to climb.

Trust, that was what they had vowed to do for each other. Was she showing trust by excluding him from her life when she needed him the most?

A new sense of purpose sent the adrenalin flowing through her system. Suddenly she knew what she had to do. She would go back to Bedales now, this minute, and pack. Then she would head straight back to Sydney and tell Rowan how she really felt, trusting him to understand what had prompted her to behave as she had towards him.

Would it be enough? She refused to let the tiniest doubt into her mind. He would trust her because he had to. He had called her the best thing to happen to him. Well, he was the best thing ever to happen to her, and she had to make sure he knew it.

Her spirits soared as she set off back to Bedales. It was just as well she knew the road by now, because she hardly saw the miles slipping past, and drove almost entirely on auto-pilot.

She was almost at the winery when she became aware of a car following uncomfortably close behind her. Experimentally, she speeded up, and the car speeded up. When she slowed, it slowed. Worried, she was forced to face the fact that it was following her. In the gathering dark, she could see only its headlights, like the eyes of some predator, and she began to shiver with apprehension.

But what could she do? This was a lonely road, with only the Bedales turn-off up ahead. Marshalling her wits, she put her foot down, as if she intended to go past the turn-off, then at the last moment she swung hard left on to the side road.

At first she thought she had outwitted her pursuer but, seconds later, the yellow lights appeared behind her again. This time, the car cut in front of her, and she was forced to pull up. Her heart beat a noisy tattoo against her chest wall as the driver got out and approached her car.

'It *is* you. Why didn't you pull up before, when I tooted at you?'

Her panic subsided. 'Rowan! I didn't hear a car horn.' She had been too preoccupied with her own thoughts, only noticing the following car at the last minute.

He helped her out of the car and held her close to him. 'God, woman, you're shaking like a leaf!'

'I thought I was being followed,' she said faintly, hardly believing that he was really here.

'You were. By me.'

'But why?'

'I was back in Sydney, waiting for you to call. When I realised you weren't going to, I decided to drive down here and try to make you see reason.'

In the half-dark, his face was all satanic planes and angles, but the light in his eyes was bright enough. 'Funny,' she said shyly, 'that's exactly what I was going to do.'

'You what?'

'I was going back to Bedales to pack, then I was coming straight on to Sydney to see you.'

'Does this mean you'll marry me?'

'If you'll have me. I realised how stupid I was being, keeping you at arm's length because I felt guilty over Trina. When I told her I had given you up, she was shocked right out of her coma.'

'So I heard. When I telephoned Bedales and got no answer, I tried the hospital and found out what had happened.'

'So you aren't angry about the way I acted?' she asked uncertainly.

'Angry at myself, maybe. I've had some time to think lately, and I discovered that trusting someone means more than controlling jealousy. It also means letting the other person decide what's best for them. If you feel we have to wait until you're ready, I won't try to change your mind.'

'But I've already changed it,' she assured him. 'I've done enough waiting for a lifetime. I also learned a few things, and one of them was how fragile life is. I want us to be together now and for always.'

In the dark, she felt something smooth and cool slide on to her finger. When Rowan had secured the ring, his hands slid upwards over her satiny skin, the strong fingers unerringly finding each tense muscle and coaxing them to relax, even while her nervous system responded by springing to vibrant life. Could one be relaxed and yet achingly alert at the same time? Rowan's touch made it possible, until she wanted to cry out with longing for him.

All the pent-up passion of the last few days came rushing out, and she moulded herself against him, twining her fingers eagerly into his hair, while her body thrust wantonly towards him.

'Oh, God, Danni,' he moaned against her mouth. Their mingled breaths tasted sweet and warm in her mouth, and her nostrils were filled with the exciting male scent of him. She drank in the cocktail of sensations, wanting to experience him with every one of her senses.

Much later, they sat in the back seat of his car, staring out across the darkened hills and valleys, content just to be together.

'I still can't believe that Trina was jealous of me,' she said at last. 'I always thought she was the lucky one.' She settled herself more comfortably in the curve of his shoulder. 'It just goes to show you that nobody gets everything they want.'

Rowan pulled her hard against him. 'What about you and me?'

His closeness sent waves of desire coursing through her, and she smiled up at him. 'There are exceptions to every rule.'

They were married in summer, among the vines of Bedales, which groaned under the weight of their soon-to-be harvested crops. Sean and Beth O'Dare had delayed their return to Ireland, and there was never a prouder father than Sean as he gave his daughter's hand to Rowan.

Fully recovered, Trina looked radiant in her bridesmaid's dress, and Danni thrilled to the adoring looks her twin kept casting at Laurie Bedford. Ever since the accident, Trina had been a frequent visitor to the vineyard. Who knew what would come of it in time?

Then Danni had eyes only for Rowan, as they exchanged marriage vows. She managed to look solemn as she promised to obey him, although his hand tightened on hers. It was much easier to agree to love one another 'till death us do part'. They had promised each other for ever, and neither of them wanted it any other way.

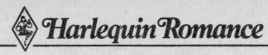 **Harlequin Romance**

Coming Next Month

2971 REMEMBER, IN JAMAICA Katherine Arthur
For three years Claire has battled with her boss over his violent temper, impossible dreams and insane schedules. Suddenly, once she agrees to the working trip in Jamaica, Terrill changes into a pussycat. Claire can't help feeling suspicious.

2972 NO LOVE IN RETURN Elizabeth Barnes
The only reason Eve has worked as a model is to pay for her brother's education. To the imperious Jackson Sinclair, however, *model* is synonymous with *gold digger*. And there seems to be no way to persuade him he's wrong.

2973 SNOWFIRE Dana James
Beth can't pass up the chance to be official photographer on an Iceland expedition, though she's stunned to find her estranged husband, Dr. Allan Bryce, as leader. Even more shocking is the realization that Allan thinks he was the injured party!

2974 SYMPATHETIC STRANGERS Annabel Murray
Recently widowed Sandra begins to build a new life for herself and her young twins by helping friends of her mother's in Kent. Yet when lord of the manor Griff Faversham pursues her, she refuses to consider marriage to another wealthy man.

2975 BED, BREAKFAST & BEDLAM Marcella Thompson
In helping Bea McNair establish an Ozark Mountain retreat for Bea's ailing friends, Janet dismisses Lucas McNair's plan to move his mother to a Little Rock retirement home. There's no dismissing Lucas, though, when he descends upon her like a wrathful God.

2976 MOWANA MAGIC Margaret Way
Ally can't deny the attraction between herself and the powerful Kiall Lancaster, despite his mistrust of her. Common sense tells her to leave. But first she determines to straighten out Kiall's chauvinistic attitude. Not an easy task!

Available in April wherever paperback books are sold, or through Harlequin Reader Service:

In the U.S.
901 Fuhrmann Blvd.
P.O. Box 1397
Buffalo, N.Y. 14240-1397

In Canada
P.O. Box 603
Fort Erie, Ontario
L2A 5X3

Harlequin Superromance

Here are the longer, more involving stories you have been waiting for...Superromance.

Modern, believable novels of love, full of the complex joys and heartaches of real people.

Intriguing conflicts based on today's constantly changing life-styles.

Four new titles every month.
Available wherever paperbacks are sold.

SUPER-1

COMING IN MARCH FROM

 Harlequin
   Superromance

Book Two of the
Merriman County Trilogy
AFTER ALL THESE YEARS
the sizzle of Eve Gladstone's
One Hot Summer continues!

Sarah Crewes is at it again, throwing Merriman County
into a tailspin with her archival diggings. In *One Hot
Summer* (September 1988) she discovered that the town
of Ramsey Falls was celebrating its tricentennial one
year too early.

Now she's found that Riveredge, the Creweses'
ancestral home and property, does not rightfully belong
to her family. Worse, the legitimate heir to Riveredge
may be none other than the disquieting Australian,
Tyler Lassiter.

Sarah's not sure why Tyler's in town, but she suspects
he is out to right some old wrongs—and some new
ones!

The unforgettable characters of *One Hot Summer* and
After All These Years will continue to delight you in
book three of the trilogy. Watch for *Wouldn't It Be
Lovely* in November 1989.

SR349-1

Have You Ever Wondered If You Could Write A Harlequin Novel?

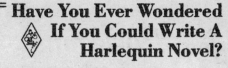

Here's great news—Harlequin is offering a series of cassette tapes to help you do just that. Written by Harlequin editors, these tapes give practical advice on how to make your characters—and your story—come alive. There's a tape for each contemporary romance series Harlequin publishes.

Mail order only

All sales final

TO: *Harlequin Reader Service*
Audiocassette Tape Offer
P.O. Box 1396
Buffalo, NY 14269-1396

I enclose a check/money order payable to HARLEQUIN READER SERVICE® for $9.70 ($8.95 plus 75¢ postage and handling) for EACH tape ordered for the total sum of $_____*
Please send:

- ☐ Romance and Presents
- ☐ American Romance
- ☐ Superromance
- ☐ Intrigue
- ☐ Temptation
- ☐ All five tapes ($38.80 total)

Signature_____
                                                                (please print clearly)
Name:_____
Address:_____
State:_____ Zip:_____

*Iowa and New York residents add appropriate sales tax.

AUDIO-H